ATTACK BY NIGHT

He moved stealthily on the guard. He was a jaguar. A cat. There was no noise. There was no warning. His mind was altered so totally that he didn't jump at the man, he *sprang* at him. With one move Billy Leaps Beeker was airborne. The knife slashed out and severed the neck, just where the jugular was exposed. His blade was his paw, its steel was his claws, the guard was his prey. . . .

Other books in the BLACK BERET series:

THE NIGHT OF
THE JAGUAR

Mike McCray

A DELL BOOK

Published by
Dell Publishing Co., Inc.
1 Dag Hammarskjold Plaza
New York, New York 10017

Dell ® TM 681510, Dell Publishing Co., Inc.

ISBN: 0-440-16235-1

Printed in the United States of America

July 1986

10 9 8 7 6 5 4 3 2 1

WFH

1

The young woman had been told that it would be done in private. Only a pair of kindly middle-aged women would have to hear her tell the most intimate details of her ordeal. They sat with her now, all three of them in comfortable stuffed chairs, coffee and tea in pots on the low table between them.

The young woman looked at the mirror and seemed to be frightened of her own reflection. She turned away quickly. It didn't matter. She could never have seen through the treated glass to know that there were at least another dozen who were eavesdropping on her.

One of them was a man the others knew only as Harry. It was his real name, certainly the only one he'd been called by for years. They would never believe that he was called only Harry because the other real name for him was Haralambos Georgeos Pappathanassiou. It was just too boring and too difficult to explain and pronounce that to anyone who wasn't a lot more than a casual acquaintance. Harry knew very few people who ever got to be more than that. None of them were here.

The room Harry stood in was small. The others with him were crowded into the space, not just by their own bodies, but also by the complex audio and video equipment they were using. The three females who were on the other side of the glass were beginning to talk now. One of the middle-aged matrons handed the girl they were calling Luisa a cup of coffee, then poured rich cream into it, lightening the color.

The conversation was being fed into the spy room over a loudspeaker. Harry could hear the three women conversing in Spanish, a language he knew not at all. It didn't matter. There was a woman standing near him who was translating their words as quickly as they were spoken.

The effect was eerie. It was like being in a movie house and listening to a foreign-language film while reading the English words that appeared on the bottom of the screen. Those written dialogues had always allowed Harry to guess at the spoken words that were coming out of the actors' mouths. But the woman in this room was too fast, and he didn't have that chance to read the screen for a moment before the character spoke.

He learned to block out the spoken Spanish, letting it just be a kind of background music, and only took in the translator's voice. It made it a little bit easier. It gave him a little distance from the pain that Luisa was describing.

My husband, Federico, was a member of the National Guard. A freedom fighter. He had devoted himself to the battle against the communists who wanted to remove the Church from El Salvador. He was a devout man. A good man.

He was assigned to be a bodyguard for Colonel Ortega y Masso about two years ago. It was, really, a reward for his service. The job had real danger, the colonel was one of the closest advisers to General Cadozza and was in constant danger. But all of El Salvador was like that. At least he had a stable post, a place near the city where we could live together.

He got me a job in the colonel's household as a maid. There were many other women who would come and go. Their jobs were not in the kitchen, however. They were his kept women. They were whores.

Luisa waved a vague hand in the air. *I am not a cloistered nun. I live in a country with many armies and many soldiers. I know such women exist and that they often have to exist. A woman needs a man to protect her from other men in war. Some of them were innocent country girls; perhaps they couldn't have known about city ways at any time. Others were widows of fallen soldiers. They knew too well the dangers of living in El Salvador without a patron.*

They seldom stayed for more than a month. When they left, most went gracefully, their pockets well lined with the colonel's money and a pat on the ass. During their time with him I knew they had made other connections with the upper echelon of the National Guard. They would not be on the streets for long.

This Angela woman was different from the very beginning. She was haughty. Some of the others had been awed by their new position as the lover of a colonel. They would put on airs. This one wasn't like that. She had the arrogance of a crown princess. She wasn't going to be the one who was kicked out of the colonel's house. I could see that. She was going to rule it for a long time.

I am no fool. A woman who has grown up in a country like El Salvador and who has lived a lifetime of civil war learns quickly, or she dies. I learned. I hated that woman. But I sensed her power. The other servants rebelled; I submitted. They were fired; I was made her personal maid.

It had its good points. Federico always traveled with the colonel. The other women never had, they were left behind in their boudoir. But Angela made sure she went with the colonel whenever possible. I, at least, got to be with my husband.

Luisa stopped again. Harry looked at her and saw an expression that was too familiar. It was the widow realizing, once more, that those times were past. There would be no more trips with her man. He was only a memory.

The momentary weakness was glossed over as Luisa hurried to continue: *But there were times when the colonel would go on certain missions on which he would not even bring Federico. They were usually to the United States, sometimes to Madrid, who knows where else?*

We would meet him in neutral places, Angela and I and Federico, just as my husband would meet him alone before. The colonel wasn't about to land in El Salvador without a bodyguard. Most often it was in Guatemala City. Other times it had been in Panama. Once, at least, it was in San José, Costa Rica.

Angela loved the trips. They gave her *opportunities to shop that were denied her at home. The woman of a National Guard colonel would never be allowed to roam the streets in San Salvador, but with Federico and me she was allowed that pleasure in the other countries.*

This time was no different. We went to Guatemala. We arrived the night before Ortega y Masso was supposed to arrive from someplace. No, *Luisa answered a question.* I don't know where. *We were staying in the El Presidente Hotel. Federico and I were anxious to be alone, to have our dinner with Angela finished so we could . . . We were a very happy couple. Federico was always promising me that someday, after the communists were defeated, we could stay in such places as the El Presidente. I laughed at the idea, but liked it very much.*

Then a man came to the table. My husband and I froze. Of course we knew who it was: the Lion of Salvador himself! The most feared man in our country, the one who it was said would eat the testicles of his defeated enemies for breakfast to prove his ferocity.

Luisa stopped again. Harry wondered what was getting to her now. The fact that her hero had turned into an enemy? Or was the memory of her husband flooding her mind and finally overpowering it? They both must have hurt, they must hurt a lot. Harry knew all about that kind of thing. He'd felt it before.

He suddenly wanted to belt the female translator who was so placidly altering the way that Luisa was talking. He could hear the pain in her Spanish speech, but the English words didn't carry any of it when they flowed out of this bureaucrat's mouth.

8

Why not? He wondered. Was this bitch just so cold that she didn't feel any of it? Or had she, too, had so much that she didn't want to let her own emotions show?

General Cadozza was well known, Luisa continued. *We all stood in deference to him. He was . . . gracious. He kissed my hand, making Federico blush with pride, as much as he did when the general shook his own. Then he greeted Angela. I knew at that moment . . . but no one could have known!* The Spanish voice was screaming: *But no one could have known. . . .* There were tears to accompany the Latin words. But the English translator might as well have been mouthing a Pepsi commercial.

Luisa regained her composure with the help of maternal pats on the back from her two keepers. There wasn't a sound in the listening room. Harry wondered if any of these jerks cared. It took a good two minutes to get Luisa back to talking.

Nothing happened that night. Nothing at all, except the look that went between them. The general, of course, had his bodyguard with him; even in Guatemala he wasn't about to take a chance at assassination. He invited us to join him in the lounge after dinner, to see a show.

The music was loud, very loud. Federico and I were relieved to be able to enjoy the show. We couldn't have heard what passed between the general and Angela in any event. Not over the band's music. So, we made believe we were sweethearts. Luisa was close to losing her composure again. But she didn't.

That night I helped Angela undress. I could understand why this woman could attract men. She is blond, unlike most other Salvadoran women. Her hair is long, she is very proud of it, vain. I would have to brush it for at least fifteen minutes every night. Her figure is trim, though her breasts are full. Her eyes are brown, though, as though they were the last remnants of her Salvadoran blood. They are mestizo eyes, not European.

The men, I suppose, thought all this was exotic. They would watch her on the streets of the cities we were in and they would want her. I saw that same expression in the eyes of General

Cadozza. I thought he was different than other men. I was wrong. Very wrong.

In the morning we all got up in time to go to the airport to meet the plane. It was one of the Learjets that the general has for his staff use. We waited, as always, at the end of the runway.

Before the plane arrived, the general's car, a big Mercedes, pulled up beside ours. I thought little of it all. I thought, if anything, that the general only wanted to have another look at the woman; that, or he was simply there as a gesture to his trusted underling. Who knew? Who cared?

The plane landed. The general and the rest of us stood with his bodyguards as the jet came to us, not to the regular terminal. That was normal. The colonel's planes never seemed to use the regular terminals in whatever airport.

No one paid attention to the bodyguard. They were always with a man like the general. Always. Now Luisa seemed to be asking for some support from the other women, some agreement that she had had no reason to suspect what was going to happen. Again, they put maternal arms around her shoulders. It gave her strength to go on still one more time.

When Colonel Ortega y Masso climbed down the stairway he was smiling, waving to Angela, his aide—my Federico—and to his own general. He walked over to us, he had his arms outstretched as though he would take the general in an embrace. He was carrying a large briefcase. I remember that.

I remember the briefcase because he tried to use it as a shield once the gunfire began. It was useless.

Now the two other women started talking quickly, asking questions and trying to get precise information. It all boiled down to one thing: Exactly what happened?

The general pulled out a handgun and began firing. He shot at the colonel and hit him in the shoulder. The colonel was shocked. All he could do was to put the case between himself and Cadozza. But by then the bodyguards had begun as well. They all had machine guns.

How many? *There were three of them.*

What did you do? *Nothing. What could I do? I stood there, not understanding what was happening and then . . .*

Yes, yes, Luisa. We know it's difficult. But you must tell us.

Then, they started shooting at Federico. My husband was a proud and loyal man. They knew that. They knew that he would fight to protect his colonel. He died. Right in front of my eyes, he died. Blood came out of the front of him, all over the place. It splattered onto the runway. But the bullets were from the back. Those machine guns sent their bullets right through my Federico's body. My dress was covered with it, even though I was far away from him. The bullets . . .

Luisa, Luisa, we must know what happened.

Yes, yes, I understand. Luisa took a deep breath and continued. *The guns shot through Federico from the back and when they came through his body, out the front, they had exploded, like land mines do on the highways in the hills. They did not just leave Federico's body, they burst from it. It was the most terrible thing I'd ever seen. His chest, it blew open, I could see his lungs, his heart, even when it was still beating.*

Now Luisa was in sobs, her breasts were heaving, but she had entered some twilight zone where the horror of what had happened couldn't reach her. Her voice changed, she simply went on.

The bullets were so plentiful and had so much power that there wasn't even time for Federico to fall down. He stood there for moments while they cut through him, exploding, like I said, and sending a torrent of blood over the runway, onto me, splattering my hair, my face, all of me. He was embracing me with his blood in those last moments.

It happened so quickly there was no time to think, to act, even to scream. Then, the machine guns stopped. There was a sudden quiet. I could only see Federico. I could only watch him as he slumped down onto the runway, dead. He was very, very dead. There was no hope.

I stood there, transfixed, desperate to find the words of a prayer to the Madonna. I searched my mind, I tried to remember the words, but I couldn't.

That was it. The sobs took over, the automatic pilot was incapable of holding back the pain and the terror any longer. Luisa was probably oblivious to the arms of the women who were holding her now, cooing to her, whispering in her ears. The voice of the translator didn't bother conveying the words of comfort. Nice things wouldn't interest anyone who would be listening to this stuff on a VCR.

Harry looked at the technicians. He wondered if any of them understood the stuff that Luisa was saying. No, he decided, you don't understand this unless you've lived through it. It would only seem to be another evening news spot to anyone who didn't understand that it *really* happened. That the blood and the pain were real.

Harry understood. He understood perfectly. That was why he had a tight, painful sensation around his chest as memories of his own resurrected themselves and called him: Remember, Harry? Huh? Remember your own wife in Vietnam? Remember the way you discovered she was a spy? How you made love to her one last time and then you took a service revolver and you shot her dead while the water was running into the bathtub? How do you forget things like that, Harry? How is Luisa ever going to forget this part of her life? Or is she going to relive it every single day for the rest of her existence on earth, just the way you do, Harry? Just the way you do. . . .

Luisa again regained her composure. The women began to ask questions again:

Didn't the Guatemalan authorities try to do anything? *I doubt they could even see. We were far away from the terminal, very far away. When it was over, when the colonel and Federico were dead, they put their bodies in the cargo part of the airplane. Then they dragged me inside the passenger compartment. There were three bodyguards with the general, they were the ones who took me. I screamed all the while, I finally had found my voice, but they only laughed.*

I couldn't understand what was happening. I was frightened for myself and I was frightened for Angela. I thought we would be killed. But, then I saw her . . .

Yes, Luisa, tell us, what did you see?

I saw her walk onto the plane after the guards had put me on it. Her dress was a light, bright yellow. It was a summer smock that she had bought the day before in Guatemala City. I thought she must be as terrified as I was, but it wasn't so. . . .

Luisa was speaking very slowly now, as though she still couldn't believe all this, weeks later, as though it had to have been a dream.

She was smiling. No, more than smiling, she was ecstatic. The blood didn't frighten her, not at all. It had made her . . . it had made her lustful. It was in her eyes. She had her arm around the general and she was staring at him. She wanted him—there, then. . . .

Are you sure? Luisa, perhaps she was in shock.

Luisa looked at her questioner and sneered. *The guards raped me. All three of them took me. I fought the first one, the one who smelled so badly and who didn't know how to do it well. He hit me, hard. Then he finished, ignoring my yells of pain.*

By then the plane was in the air. The second one took off his pants and mounted me. I had no fight left. I had no reason to resist. I let him. Now I was only worried that I would be hit again. I lay there on the floor of the aisle with my legs open and could only think of Federico, dead.

I was hardly even aware that this one was inside me. He had ripped off my blouse and was pawing my breasts. But I ignored him. I looked around the plane. It was so luxurious, so modern, it seemed incredible that this was happening to me in such a place.

I saw her. She wasn't resisting, not at all. She was on her knees, between his legs, she had him in her mouth. She was doing it with joy. Her dress was dropped open and, while I watched her, she took the general's hands and brought them down onto her naked breasts. She moaned with pleasure.

13

Then the last one climbed on me, laughing like the other two. He was the cruelest of all, the worst of the three, because of what he did. He was kind. He was smiling at me, daring me to ignore him. He did it well, as though we were lovers. I couldn't help it, oh, Mother of God, I couldn't help it. . . .

No one touched Luisa this time, they knew she was going to go on eventually. She had to tell someone about this part of it. All too obviously it was a confession; she had to relieve herself of the burden of her guilt.

I responded, she began again through more tears. *I couldn't help but respond. He was good at it, saying filthy things in my ear, telling me that I felt . . . He told me he liked me. At least he didn't hurt me, not physically.*

He did it for a long time. When he was finished, he gave me a small kiss on my forehead and lifted me up. He took me to a seat and apologized when he put on metal restraints to keep me from moving; otherwise, he told me, they would kill me. I let him do that.

Luisa lifted her hands, indicating that the story was over. The questions flew at her again. *No, I never saw them again after we landed at San Salvador. Yes, I stayed with my captor for a month. I had no place else to go. I had no money. The colonel's house had to be closed. Certainly, Angela never sent for me. I was alone in San Salvador! Don't you know what that means? To be a woman alone in a city full of fighting and armies and men who have only the allegiance of staying with the man they think will save them? I had no choice!*

Then, he let me go. He gave me a little money and a set of false papers and told me I should leave. He had a wife, it turns out. She was coming to the capital to be with him and his kept woman, his whore, couldn't be there when she arrived. That's when I killed him. —

How? I took a knife that night when he was asleep. He had betrayed me, never telling me about this marriage of his. I was not his wife, I know that, but he was supposed to be my protector

14

during the war. He had no right to leave me defenseless in a city like San Salvador.

I took a knife and I stabbed him many, many times in the chest. I took his money and the papers and I came here, to Mexico. I had a sister here. I thought I would be safe. But then last week, she was murdered. That's why I came to you, because I am sure they thought my sister was me. They were after me, after more revenge. I need protection.

"Jesus Christ!" The translator suddenly said. Harry turned and looked at her. "What a story. The guy saves her life, gives her money and papers, and then she kills him! I hope to hell we're going to just turn her back over to the Salvadorans. She deserves their kind of justice."

The translator was young, perhaps twenty-five. She was not attractive and she had bad skin, the pockmarks of two and a half decades of acne were cruelly obvious in the low light of the half-lit room. Harry looked at her and let two emotions fight it out between themselves: One, the urge to pull the bitch's hair and smack her face for having no compassion, no understanding of the cruelty of war. Two, the desire to laugh in her face. If this were a war zone and she were in Luisa's position, she'd never have gotten the one month reprieve to regain her senses and have the courage to kill her captor. She wasn't pretty enough for a war-hardened soldier to bother with.

Harry didn't have to let his emotions choose a course of action. A door opened, sending a shaft of bright light into the enclosed space. "Harry, have you heard enough?"

"Yeah," he said. He walked toward the open doorway and went through it, not caring that a dozen people had turned their heads, wondering just who the huge man was.

No one had thought much about Harry during the recital they were recording. They had all stared at him when he had first shown up. That was usual. Harry was a big man, six feet two and over two hundred pounds that had been molded into pure muscle in the past couple of years. He was in his middle thirties, but his body seemed younger and his face seemed older.

He was the kind of man you'd notice, but one you couldn't quite figure out.

He had stood in that room in a sea of personal emotions, but none of the others had known that. They were aware of only one: sadness. A deep, agonizing sadness that seemed to be a part of him no matter how well put together his muscles were or how expensive his clothes were.

Luisa's story hadn't caused that. The others had seen it and sensed it well before the woman had walked into the room with the two-way mirror. Her tale was only another grain of sand added to the mountain of grief that he seemed to be carrying around with him.

The woman who'd called him was as different as possible from Harry. She was short, blond, blue eyed, and everything about her was younger than she was—though Harry realized he didn't know how old she really was.

Her name was Delilah. She was someone in Washington, Harry did know that. She had an office where she could be reached. She had a lot of information. She could arrange a lot of things. This was only one example of the fun times that Delilah could provide for men like Harry. She'd proven that many times before.

They left the building in silence. There was a limousine waiting for them. Harry was glad it was a Cadillac. He wouldn't have wanted to ride in a stretch Mercedes so quickly after hearing Luisa. He cared about things like that. He would have done it, if those were the orders, but he wouldn't have liked it one single bit.

They rode to the airport outside the Mexican border city where the interview had taken place. Harry's luck didn't keep up. The plane waiting for them was a Lear. It was probably the same kind of craft that had taken Luisa on her nightmare journey.

Silently—they hadn't spoken a word since leaving the interrogation—Harry and Delilah climbed up the stairs. Harry realized that he'd been right. This would have been exactly the same model jet the Salvadoran woman had flown in. There was only one Lear model that fit the general description.

He sat in one of the luxurious chairs and fastened his seat belt. He listened to the familiar whine of the jet engines as they revved up. Then there was the tug of the acceleration. Soon they were airborne. A steward appeared out of nowhere and offered him a drink. He could have used one, but didn't want to have it on his breath when he got to the home base.

He looked out the window and saw that they'd climbed over the clouds. He could look down and see the puffy white mounds and he was even able to think that they were pretty. After having heard Luisa, he was amazed that he could think anyone was pretty. He certainly didn't want to think that about Delilah these days. Maybe she was, but the stuff she brought to them never had a nice appearance. Not ever.

As the plane moved northward, Harry was consumed with one thought. *Why me?*

It wasn't a plaintive whine. It was a simple and straightforward question, one he'd asked himself many times.

Why me?

He realized that Luisa had never asked that question. She had simply accepted her fate. She had grown up in a country constantly hemorrhaged by war. Things happened to people in war. Men were killed. Women were raped. Some people escaped, but few.

Harry asked a lot of questions. He asked that question because his life and his experiences went far beyond the limited personal traumas of a person like Luisa.

He had grown up in a Greek family on the South Side of Chicago. He had just been a regular guy, a little bigger, a little stronger, a little quieter, than most. That was all. He'd gone into the service during the Vietnam War. That was what a Greek kid from the South Side did.

Then he'd slipped into the special training the Navy had for the heavy stuff. He became a SEAL. One night, when he was out drinking with his pal, Marty Appelbaum, they'd met up with a half-breed Cherokee, a Marine sergeant. That was the first moment when the question became real. *Why did Beeker find me?*

But he did. Billy Leaps Beeker had found Marty and Harry and the next thing they'd known they were part of a special unit called the Black Berets. They did things in Nam that no one ever heard about. They were the ones who worked outside the codes of the Geneva Convention. The ones who didn't care that there were little imaginary lines that meant they were crossing forbidden international boundaries. They did it all.

When they were done, it turned out that they were really done. Nothing that they'd accomplished was recorded, not even their own years in the war. Someone pushed a button in Washington and the Black Berets were erased. Totally and unalterably; they had never existed.

They hadn't known that then. Instead they had come back to the United States and they had tried to fit in, return to the civilian life. Harry had taken over a bar on the South Side, a place where working stiffs came and tried to wash away the grime of their shifts in the mills and factories that polluted the air all around them.

He'd stayed there, living in an apartment on the second floor by himself, never drinking with his customers, but always going to bed alone with a fifth of Scotch. He existed, that was the best word he could find. He existed that way for years, letting his mind go, letting his body go, letting his dreams torment him at night.

Then, Beeker had returned. He wanted the group together again. The team, the men who had never made it back into the civilized ranks of American society. They had all just existed, the same way Harry had.

The first time had been an excuse. They were just going to get together again to go into the jungles of Laos and find a friend of theirs who had been left behind. Or so they thought. That was all, just a little deadly reunion of some fighting guys from the war who were going to rescue a buddy.

18

But the buddy was a sham. He'd died long before. They were being used by someone. They found out how. Then they found him. Then they killed him. But they learned lessons from the adventure.

The first one was the most important. They belonged together. They had to be together. Life outside the Black Berets was meaningless. They were just walking wounded in the civilian life. As a team, back in shape, back to their jobs, they could survive, relive what it meant to be men, not puppets.

That was the second lesson. They weren't going to be anyone's puppets. The Black Berets were their own men. They did things because they were right. Or they did things because they got money. Or they did things because people forced their hand. But they didn't act just because some tight-assed bureaucrat in the Pentagon got hot thinking about a communist conspiracy or because one dude thought he could use them to get rid of a little competition. They did things they chose for their own reasons, their own income, or their own defense. That was all.

His mind went down the roster of the men whom Billy Leaps had brought back together again.

There was the leader, of course. Beeker, the sometimes aloof, sometimes arrogant, always trustworthy decision maker. The kind of man who had been born to go to Lejeune and who had adored boot camp. The kind who had his first high inside Marine haircut and never let a single strand grow any longer again in his life. The one who had no weakness, showed no emotions, displayed no fear—until the kid came along.

Tsali wasn't one of the regulars. He was only a seventeen-year-old, full-blooded Cherokee, something so rare the government should have declared him a living national landmark all by himself. Beeker had saved his life from some rednecks a couple years ago. He'd saved his soul by taking him out of the welfare system that was designed to turn adolescents into juvenile delinquents. He'd adopted him legally and given the kid a new name, Tsali, after some ancient Cherokee warlord.

There was Cowboy. Sherwood Hatcher was the real name,

but like Harry's own, it was so seldom used that Cowboy had more than once looked at his pilot's license and wondered how he'd gotten hold of someone else's wallet, someone with a weird name like that. Cowboy had been in the cavalry in the war. He was born to be a flyer, just as Beeker was born to be a Marine.

His daddy had brought him up in a traveling airshow that roamed through the Southwest, playing county fairs in Arkansas, rodeos in Texas, festivals in Oklahoma. The guy was probably conceived a couple thousand feet up in the air, at least it would have made sense if he had been. He never seemed comfortable on the ground. He flew as much as he could, whatever he could, as well as any man had dreamed of.

Cowboy probably would have been happy just doing for the rest of his life what his daddy had done, but there were the new jets that drew him. A man who would have been perfectly happy living his life as a function illiterate, Cowboy had looked at those jets and asked someone what he had to do to fly them. Go to college, was the answer. So Cowboy studied as though he were some kind of Rhodes Scholar, got admitted to Texas A&M, and was on his way to Nam to jockey helicopters and fighters before the ink was wet on his diploma.

Roosevelt Boone never went to college. He was another one of the team. Rosie was one of the biggest, blackest men that Harry had ever seen. He was strong as a bull, fast as Beeker, smart as Cowboy, and as mysterious as Harry. Rosie always had a smile on his face, a big smile. It covered something. He had to be hiding something. When the other guys had found him to get him to rejoin the team, Rosie was working in the morgue of the Newark General Hospital, where his duties were to peel the skin off cadavers so it could be used in bandages for burn victims.

Rosie was handsome, like a movie star, those new black ones, but he was frightening in some ways. There were many women who were attracted to him, that was obvious. But others would see something else in him besides his physical appeal. Those women backed off, quickly. They wanted nothing to do with the man who held that secret—whatever it was.

Then, of course, there was Marty. Martin Appelbaum from New Jersey. Skinny, runty, asthmatic Marty, who was a constant pain in the ass to everyone about everything. If Tsali ever proved his perfection it would be because he didn't seem to mind Appelbaum. Of course, Tsali was mute, so he never had to come up with any conversation to answer Appelbaum's endless bragging and complaining. He only had to stand there and smile. Maybe, Harry thought, Tsali could turn off his hearing just the way some childhood disease had turned off his speech? Who knew.

Marty was Harry's sidekick, actually. It had begun in the SEALs. Harry never had understood just how or why that had happened. He supposed, in some ways, that his life had been such shit that the added irritation of letting someone like Marty think he had a friend was nothing, a little gift to give to the world. Whatever, they were friends.

It was amazing that Marty was part of the Black Berets. Amazing, because he caused everyone so much trouble and annoyance. But there was a reason for it. Each of them had his skill. Beeker was the leader. Tsali was the peace-keeper. Harry knew about small arms. So did Rosie, who also knew as much about medicine necessary on the battlefield as any M.D.

And Marty knew about bombs.

When they'd found him this last time, when they called him back to join the Black Berets again, Appelbaum was blowing up buildings in St. Louis. It was a perfect location for him, the one city in the United States with, proportionately, the largest number of deserted and worthless buildings. Marty had mastered the art of implosion, the type of demolition that caused a structure to fall in on itself rather than out in a way that could have hurt people.

Of course, Marty could have reversed the process. He could have leveled the whole city of St. Louis as easily as he so carefully protected all but the designated targets. Marty could do almost anything with bombs. He had once said that a pack of cards, a bottle of gasoline, and a rubber band were all he needed to do in the Empire State Building. No one doubted him.

Marty bragged about a lot of things. He mouthed off about women the others would swear were nonexistent and he grossly exaggerated his claims of battlefield glory. But he never, ever, had to boast about bombs. No matter how extravagant his claims were about explosives, they were probably correct. You learned that about Marty.

Why me?

Harry sighed again. Why shouldn't he be living on a farm in Louisiana with four other Vietnam Vets and an adolescent, mute Cherokee? Why shouldn't he be traveling in a Learjet on his way back home with a woman whose only name was Delilah and who had information and contacts that bespoke of enormous power and influence? Why shouldn't he have been listening to the testimony of a woman who'd been raped—in every sense of the word—of her body, of her husband, of her love, of her dignity?

Why not? *Why not me?*

The Lear flew on and Harry began to doze. A dream came into his head. It was something to do with being happy, an emotion that was so rare in his life that he welcomed it in his dream. He was happy and he was in love. It was in Vietnam and there was a woman. They were getting married. They were marching under a canopy of swords and they were smiling. But then, he was holding a revolver in his hand and she was kneeling in front of him, turning her head to see him. She didn't ask, *Why me?* She knew. She also understood that he had no choice. He had discovered that she was a spy for the Viet Cong and that she would have done him in as well. He only hoped that she would have had as much trouble pulling the trigger as he did. Then he shot her. It was the end of his love. He would never know it again. He had been forced to kill his own wife in war.

Why me?

22

Harry woke with a start when the plane began to descend. He looked out the window, not sure how long he'd been asleep. The last time he'd checked, they'd been over the Gulf of Mexico. But now the land beneath them was green. The careful geometry of farmland cut up the landscape into neat sections. It was Louisiana. The plane was headed toward Shreveport. The farm where the Black Berets lived was nearby.

Rosie was always joking that Beeker expected to buy the entire state, and then start on Oklahoma. The guy had a fetish for land. It was as though it was the only thing in the world he trusted, the ownership of his own land. They lived in the middle of a spread that was well over a thousand acres by now. It was so large that they'd all stopped counting the size of the new purchases. There was no reason to bother. The number would only grow as soon as Beeker could arrange for another buy.

If the pilot had wanted to—or had to—he could have landed right at the doorstep to their house. Cowboy had often brought in planes like this. The long, paved driveway was deceptive. If you weren't studying it carefully, you wouldn't have realized that it was designed as a runway.

But this was a perfectly legal, registered flight in an apparently perfectly legal, registered airplane. This time they'd use the Shreveport Regional Airport. This time there wasn't any need for deception.

He'd be home soon. That simple fact had an impact on Harry. He was going to be home, and home was an armed camp, a military compound as sophisticated as any in the world. It was a place inhabited only by trained warriors. It was his life, it was his destiny. It was the only home he could think of ever wanting. Or at least it was the only home he could think of ever having.

2

"Why us?" Billy Leaps Beeker was sitting in a chair in front of the large fireplace. There wasn't a flame. The Louisiana summer was too hot and too humid to bother with anything that would give off more heat. The stone floor of the living room was, in fact, the only really cool thing around. He was apparently hard at work, concentrating on beading a chest ornament in the traditional Indian style.

He wouldn't look up and talk directly to Delilah. She was used to this kind of treatment from him and didn't seem to let it bother her. She took a seat on a nearby couch and pulled out a cigarette. She lighted it with a gold lighter and inhaled. The wave of the ember sent Marty running for an ashtray for her.

The men in the house didn't smoke—not even cigarettes. Nor, at least at home, did they drink alcohol or use any drugs. In this house—in Billy Leaps Beeker's house—they were in constant training. If he had his way, they would be in training outside it as well. But there were limits to his control, as much as he hated to admit it.

"Wine, Del?" the little blond man asked solicitously as he brought over the ashtray. She nodded and he went to fulfill her request. The presence of the beautiful woman in their usually all-male enclave brought out the chivalrousness in the men. Beeker hated that. He suspected, probably correctly, that she did it on purpose just in order to show him that she had her own powers to match some of his.

She waited until the wine had been delivered and only then began to talk. "General Cadozza can't be touched by anyone else."

"That's sure as hell true!" Marty exclaimed. "The Lion of Salvador is the primo stud in Central America. No one's going to get in his way. If it weren't for him the commies would have started walking up and down Latin América years ago. He's the first and last defense the U.S. of A. has against—"

"Marty, I want you to kill him." Delilah ended Appelbaum's rambling speech with a quick, decisive statement.

"You want us to take out the best friend America has?" Appelbaum was stunned. He lived in a world of comic-book right and wrong—they are bad and we are good. The communists are out to get us and we have to get them first. General Cadozza, according to every right-wing politician and commentator in the country, was on our side first and foremost. He was our surrogate in the brutal Salvadoran civil war. "How could you want us to take out the most American spic that ever lived?"

Delilah looked at Marty and felt a little sorry that she'd created such a disappointment for the guy. She might as well tell him that Superman was a Nazi; Batman was a crook; Captain America was a closet homosexual.

"What I want, Marty, is for the team to go down there and eliminate the major source of smuggled drugs entering this country."

"Cadozza?" Beeker finally looked up. "Drugs?"

"It's the way he's been financing his army. The Congress wouldn't give any real funds for arms, for soldiers' pay. They won't bankroll a right-wing coûp, that's the bottom line. He

25

had to find a way to get hold of the massive amounts of cash that he needs. Some people in Washington came up with the perfect solution. They put the screws on the usual sources of cocaine and heroin, they finally went to work and dried up the supply, then they turned all their new friends in the underworld on to the only trustworthy source left. General Cadozza."

Beeker went back to his handiwork. He'd heard it all before. There'd been private armies in Indochina—all over Southeast Asia—that had financed themselves by the same means.

"So what?" Beeker said. "What's the big deal? Your friends want to give the franchise to someone new? Let them."

"It's not that simple. You know it isn't." She put out her cigarette and sipped her wine. "There's been a secret meeting among some of the world's leaders. It seems that many of them have finally realized that drugs are more than a simple street-crime problem. They're understanding that the entire moral fabric of this country—and others—is being destroyed by chemicals. They've agreed that the problem has gotten out of hand."

"So?" Beeker continued being difficult. "What's the problem, then? If they've all agreed to eliminate the traffic, they could do it. So long as they all agreed."

"They have," Delilah said, staring at Beeker with an odd intensity. "They *all* have agreed. But some of the operations have gotten too large for simple police action. The source has to be eradicated. That was the agreement at the highest levels."

"But it's not just right-wingers like Cadozza who're doing this. You know that. The left wing gets its money the same way —in Colombia, in Ecuador . . ."

"They'll be taken care of."

"By who? Is that the assignment after this one?" Beeker was becoming more antagonistic.

"No. That part is going to be taken care of by the only other person in the Western Hemisphere who has as much ability as you do to accomplish the mission."

"Who's that?" Beeker demanded.

"Castro."

They all froze, stunned by her revelation. Beeker put aside his craftwork and stood up. The other men shifted, their body language telling all that they were paying much closer attention than ever before.

"You want us to take care of Cadozza as part of a scheme that includes Castro? Are you crazy, lady? Do you think that we're going to help that son of a bitch—"

Delilah cut him off. She was one of the few people who ever would have dared to do that. "The meeting where all this was decided was held only a week ago.

"It wasn't the first time. There was a period when any domestic flight in the United States was in danger of being hijacked. There were as many unscheduled hops to Havana from Miami as there were scheduled flights to New York. Castro was—and he still is—the most hated and the most dangerous political enemy this country has ever had so close to its own borders. But there are some times when the mutual interests of Cuba and the United States are close enough that . . . arrangements can be made between the two countries.

"They're never formal. We don't even have diplomatic relations with one another. But there are opportunities in certain places—dinner parties at the Swedish embassy in Geneva to which the American and the Cuban ambassadors to Switzerland just happened to be invited—along with their French, British, and Russian counterparts. When they all agree that hijacking is no longer in their best common interests, it stops cold. Haven't you noticed how safe the American—and the Cuban—domestic skies have been for quite a while?

"Now they've agreed that the wild cards they've been playing have begun to boomerang. There were some fools in Washington who thought that the creative financing they were providing their friends—people like Cadozza—was just the ticket. They forgot to ask their counterparts at the FBI what the social cost of unlimited cocaine would be to America. They've gotten the message.

27

"Their equivalents in Havana and Moscow are getting the same messages. Now, everyone's agreed to act. A little bit too late, though."

"What the fuck does that mean?" Beeker asked suddenly.

"It means that now that everyone's investigating, they're discovering that it had all gotten out of hand in any event. The money you can get from drugs isn't penny ante. It's big, very big. Some of the people involved have gotten very, very much attached to their incomes. Cadozza's one of them.

"He's still the head of his own army in El Salvador. But it's totally out of control now. It's a fiefdom; he's carved up a bit of the country as a duty-free port for his own use. He's so powerful the newly elected government is powerless to intrude. He wasn't content with just delivering the goods to his new friends in the United States, he's become a partner.

"The entire façade of General Cadozza is a sham. He's become, simply, a mobster. But the American people don't know that. They still think he's a hero. He got five honorary degrees in this country last June. We can't appear to be taking him out. We can't look like the bad guys. We can't turn popular opinion against him.

"Castro has the same problem with his . . . friends in Colombia. The entire world looks on them as one of the most wonderful set of freedom fighters in history. He can't have his commandos go in and get rid of them. Not at all. He has to eliminate them in a way that will create a façade of their heroism, leave their position intact."

"So you and Castro have to get rid of your little creations in El Salvador and Colombia—and God knows where else. But you can't just get rid of them, you have to find a way that doesn't hurt their reputation? You bureaucrats are the biggest, dumbest, most stupid . . . What the hell do you expect to do?" Beeker was standing now, his darkly tanned face reddening with anger and frustration.

"We all expect to do the only sane thing. We expect to take out the mobsters who've suddenly become such a problem. Ev-

28

eryone will take out their own creations. But in their place we'll leave martyrs."

"Martyrs?"

"Yes. It's simple. Cadozza will be finally defeated by a left-wing terrorist group. His counterpart in Colombia by a right-wing military organization. Both governments will have to react appropriately to the change in the balance of power, which will actually leave both of them in better shape. And the problem will be solved."

"You mean that Cadozza, the Lion of Salvador, the guy who's fought every red in Latin America's history and won, is going to lose?" It was all breaking Appelbaum's heart. How could his hero lose to those guys. "Who's going to do it? Who's got the balls to take on the Lion of Salvador?" Appelbaum asked, his chest pumping out, his face flushing pink with emotion.

"I think the Chequipac Liberation Front will finally do the deed." Delilah said, again taking a sip of wine.

"Who the hell are they? Huh? I mean, I never heard about them and I read everything I can about Cadozza. Who's this Checkerpack thing anyway, that they're going to come out of left field and put away the Lion of Salvador? Huh?" Marty was being swept up in his emotions. If his hero was going to fall, then the enemy had better be—

"You are the Chequipac Liberation Front." Delilah smiled.

"We are?" Marty fell back in his chair.

"You are a little-known, militant leftist organization, one of dozens operating in the hills of El Salvador. You have become much more active lately. In fact, you'll be reported on *The CBS Morning News* tomorrow morning. Your strength is building, showing a definite threat to the power of General Cadozza. He will be told that he must eliminate you if he expects to continue to operate. I'm sure he'll try. Then, you'll act."

"We're a *liberation front?*" When Marty asked that question it came out as a dreaded statement, a deep and dark, horror-filled thought.

"Yes, Marty. You are. And you're one of the most unreason-able leftist groups in the country. I even understand that you got your training from the PLO. In fact, you've been armed by the Russians with AK-47's and surface-to-air missiles of the latest design. Their presence in El Salvador is going to be a major concern to Washington. And to the right-wing forces in this country who have given Cadozza his aura of respectibility. Such a thing cannot be allowed in El Salvador, not at all. He'll have to move to get rid of you.

"Could I have some more wine, please?" Delilah smiled and held out her glass.

"You mean to tell me that you want us to go into the jungles of El Salvador, where there are already God knows how many armies fighting it out with one another, and you want us to make believe that we're a screwed-up left-wing organization, and you expect us to move on the army that Cadozza has gath-ered and—"

"You won't be making believe that you're a liberation front, Beeker. I told you, CBS is going to say you *are* a liberation front. You exist. It'll be on television tomorrow morning. There is no finer proof. Maria Shriver herself is going to report on you.

"Besides, it's hardly screwed up, as you call it. It's a Native American organization."

"You bitch," Beeker hissed out at her for daring to bring in his Indian heritage. "You goddamn bitch."

3

"What about the women?" Harry asked Delilah.

They'd fought about the idea of going to El Salvador undercover for hours. It was late. They were all tired. They'd make their decision tomorrow. But before he could think about it any more, Harry had to know why he'd been taken to Mexico.

"Luisa has been given sanctuary by a convent. She'll probably spend the rest of her life there. She's got a right to be frightened. She also has a lot to think about and to get over— her husband, killing the guard, watching . . ."

"And the other one? The Angela she talked about?" Harry didn't want to hear about Luisa's life of penitence and sorrow. He could have guessed that beforehand.

"I wanted you all to know about Cadozza. What he's really like. I knew her story before you heard it. I didn't know if you'd believe it if one of you didn't hear it from her own lips. I had to show you that this is really a beast, a man gone wild with power. He is, Harry. He really is. The best way to know it is to listen to the people who get closest to him. When he's onstage on a talk show in this country or when he's in uniform reviewing his troops, he looks awfully good. The Boy Scouts of America love him. But when he's seen up close, he's a bastard."

Harry stared at Delilah. He thought he should get mad at her. At least he had an answer to one of the small parts of his question: *Why me?* He had been chosen, he knew at once, because he was the one who'd remember everything Luisa said. It would be etched in his mind forever.

He'd been chosen because it would give him motivation to go on the assignment. Harry was the quiet one, the one who didn't always need to be in battle, who didn't always want to be toting a rifle, but one who'd rather . . . But once he'd heard the story, he'd be ready. Delilah knew that.

The opening had been so simple. There was a possible assignment. She had to deliver some facts and show some background. There was to be a briefing in Mexico. Why not send Harry down to hear it? Why not? *Why not me?*

Marty would have had a hard time believing that his star stud, Cadozza, was such a bad guy. Cowboy was always falling in love with Latin women. When he'd heard the description of Angela's beauty and sexuality, he'd just have wanted her. Rosie didn't need to have the motivation. Beeker wouldn't have left the country on a speculation. But Harry? Sure, Harry would go down to Mexico on Delilah's Learjet and listen to the torment of a Salvadoran woman and hear about the perfidy of men in war, and Harry would care.

He wasn't so complicated after all, he decided. Because Delilah had guessed right. He did care. He cared with that part of his soul that still functioned. She was right. He wanted to kill Cadozza for what had happened. And, probably just as important, he wouldn't give a good damn about Angela if he saw her and she was, in fact, the most beautiful woman in the world. If he had to, he'd kill her too.

Harry felt defeated already. The battle he'd be going into wouldn't matter. He put a hand to his forehead and nodded. He understood. "I think I'll go to bed now."

No one spoke to him as he stood up and moved out of the large, well-furnished living room. He walked past the large baronial dining table and into a corridor of unadorned concrete blocks, just like those on the outside walls.

The house was plain, of course it was; a house for men didn't need a woman's decoration. The living quarters up front were richly furnished in a highly masculine way. They were at least close to the way that you'd think that very, very wealthy men like the Black Berets would live.

But the small rooms that lined this hallway showed the other side of the group. There were six of them, one for each of the men and another for Tsali. At the end was a communal showerroom and lavatory. The cubicles that housed each man's private space were Spartan. They held only a bed, a bureau, a closet, a single table, and a cotlike military bed. That was all a fighting man needed.

The decor of the living and dining rooms was only a front, the only touch of elegance in their lives. These bedrooms were their reality. The quarters of warriors.

Harry stood in front of his door for a moment. He hadn't heard anyone following him, but there was suddenly a body next to his. He turned and saw Tsali beside him.

The boy had long black hair that broke over his shoulders Cherokee fashion. He was wearing camouflage pants and a simple olive-drab T-shirt. He was already nearly as tall as Harry, at least as tall as Beeker's six feet. He was skinny, though; even after all the good food and toughening up he'd had on the farm, the leftovers of childhood poverty showed in his thinness.

Harry reached over and tousled the kid's hair. He was still young enough to do that to. "What do you think?"

The Black Berets will go. Tsali couldn't speak, but all the Berets had learned to translate his sign language in order to understand him.

"Yeah, we'll go." Harry said, turning the doorknob.

Tsali put a hand on his shoulder to stop him. Harry looked over at the boy.

It's the right thing.

"Is it?" Harry asked.

Tsali nodded emphatically.

Because he believed Delilah? Because he wanted action? Because . . .

Because warriors go to battle. With that, Tsali turned and left.

Harry watched him walking back to the living room and understood that the answer didn't make him feel any better. It made him feel much worse.

Rosie would go. He already knew he wanted to go. He was standing in the shower and soaping himself up, singing to himself. He'd go for a very simply reason. There were people who were bringing the bad dope into this country and he wanted to stop it.

Not for the yuppies who wanted to play cool and snort their coke. Let them burn their noses off. Not for the men like himself and Cowboy who knew about the joys of a little toke or a little toot. They'd get theirs somehow. But for the ones who were going to turn thirteen with a needle in their elbow in Harlem. For the babies that were going to be born in Watts with a heroin addiction their only heritage. For the sweet young girls who would have sung in their church choir, but couldn't 'cause they were still in bed, sleeping after a hard night hustling on their backs to get enough money for the one thing in this world that made them feel as good as their mamas told them Jesus should.

Rosie had grown up with the idea of the Revolution in the black ghettoes of America. He'd seen the Revolution, all right. It was made up of burned-out blocks of middle-class black houses in Detroit and broken black dreams in Alabama. It was dead children who'd been set up by "organizers" to take the heat from the cops.

He'd seen it all. The only real revolution Rosie thought about these days was the one that would stop the flow of poison into the lives and neighborhoods of young black people.

34

He rinsed off and grabbed a towel to dry himself. The life here on the farm was getting too boring, anyway. They were rich, but did little with their money. Every once in a while he and Cowboy would go off to Vegas or Miami Beach or someplace else and they'd have a party. But it was always too boring and too long away from home. They seemed to be coming back earlier and earlier. They needed something. This was the ticket. He only wondered if the others would do it.

Just as he'd wound the towel around his waist and gotten ready to go back to his room, Marty Appelbaum burst into the shower room. "Do you believe that shit? Can you believe it?"

Marty tore off his own towel and stood under one of the shower heads and turned it on. Rosie studied the little man. He was thin, thinner than Tsali. He wasn't that tall, only about five nine, and he was as pale as a white man could be in Louisiana in the summertime. But Rosie knew, as all the Black Berets did, that Marty was as strong as a bull. There had to be some strange chemicals of his own coursing through his bloodstream. Because when Appelbaum got pissed, you had better stand out of the way. He often took on men three times his size and did them in.

But now it sounded like Marty was going to have as much trouble with this assignment as Rosie had feared. "You think it's a bad idea, huh?" Rosie asked.

"Bad idea? You mean to go to take care of Cadozza? *Hell no!* That asshole deserves it! He deserves to see what real American men believe in."

"Oh, yeah?" Rosie leaned against the door frame. He couldn't figure this one out.

"Hell, letting all those American kids think he was a bigshot, big-cheese hero when he's nothing but a gangster. Hell . . ." Marty's voice trailed off in a tone of contempt.

Now Rosie understood. Marty felt betrayed. That was his own motivation. Cadozza had lied to him—personally. He was ready to settle the score.

"So, you think we should go?"

"Of course I do." Marty was scrubbing his pink flesh so hard there were lines, almost welts, of red on his stomach and chest. "Besides, I think you and me will make the best-looking Indians of all!" He lifted his arm in a mock victory salute, displaying the skin underneath. Rosie noticed, disbelievingly, that it was even paler there than on the rest of his body.

"You and me, Indians? This is going to be a story!" With that, Rosie let out a booming laugh and turned and walked out, ready to go to bed at last.

4

They would go. He knew they would. All of them had individually decided that last night. Their arguments against the assignment had been weak and easily pushed aside. Each one had a reason.

Billy Leaps Beeker looked out over his land from the front steps of his house. He wondered just what his own decision was based on. Any sane man would just stay here in Louisiana. He watched the humidity rise off the ground. You could do that in Shreveport in the summer. The evening had brought only a little cool, but that had produced a chance for the grass to capture some moisture. Now, with the first harsh rays of sunlight, it was evaporating, leaving the atmosphere in waves that were visible to the naked eye. It would break a hundred degrees today. He could already feel it.

Any sane man would stay indoors in this brutal weather. Any man who had as much land as Beeker did would turn on an air-conditioner—if he had one, which Beeker didn't—and he'd sit and drink gin-and-tonics for a while. He wouldn't go off to some two-bit country in Central America and . . .

But he would. Beeker knew he would. He'd do it for the things he thought were right. He'd do it because there was no other way for the situation to be handled. Anyone else would be caught up in constantly restricting rules, congressional overviews, military reviews. A plan had gone wrong. There was nothing new about that. Some wise-ass in the Pentagon had miscalculated—again. Instead of winning a battle that should have been taken care of years ago, they'd created a cancer.

Another warlord had gone too far, tasted too much of the profits he could make if he gave up his ideals. Another revolutionary had been coopted. It happened all the time. And when it happened, there was no way for this country to strike back except to use some extraordinary force. That was what they were—extraordinary and forceful.

It was their continuing role. They'd played it in Nam and they'd played it in a half-dozen other countries around the globe. Now it would be El Salvador. No matter how much they tried to deny it, they were once again faced with the proof that their journeys weren't going to end, not for a long time.

He could smell her before she spoke. Her perfume was subtle, never crass the way so many other women's scents were. But it was pervasive. It overpowered even the odors of the nearby forest and the summer blooms. She was close. He didn't have to turn to see that. Her aroma told him.

He felt himself harden. They hadn't talked much after the meeting last night, and what conversation there had been didn't have a thing to do with military operations. She had come to his room without asking him or waiting to be asked.

She hadn't waited to be seduced either. She had stood in the small cubicle and she'd simply and easily removed her clothing, standing naked and unashamed in front of him and expecting his approval. He'd given it by ripping off his own clothing and, for once, not folding it with military precision.

They hadn't minded the summer heat. They had seemed to

welcome it. They'd made love as though it were the only thing for them to do and as though they were the only ones who could have done it with each other. Maybe it was true.

Maybe, Beeker realized, it came down to those three elemental emotions: Make love to the woman you need; teach the son you adore; fight the battle you have to. That was it. That was a man's life. Stripped of all the nice things and the civilizing drives and the conventions of society.

Had all this been just a long process to get him to return to the level of an animal? He wondered, because as much as he tried, he couldn't think of a damn thing that separated him from the primal needs of a panther.

Her hand came out and rested on his shoulder. It was soft. Everything about her seemed that way. Everything about her was so supple and vulnerable. Everything about him was hard and demanding. His muscles were etched on his body. There wasn't a spare ounce of fat on his torso. There wasn't a single determined muscle on hers.

But there were other places where they met as equals. Their minds, for one. That was the most important. Her mind could run his ragged, could make his turn inside out with desire and need. It was his one open wound, his thoughts and the way that woman got into them.

"Breakfast?" she asked.

He snorted. Right. There was one more primal need. Food. Toss the panther some bloody red meat, let him chew it, and let him rip it off the bones of his prey. He'd forgotten that one. Foolish, he shouldn't have.

"Yeah." He turned and began to walk through the doorway again. But she wouldn't budge. Her breasts pressed against his chest and stopped him; their pliant mass seemed to exude even more smell than the rest of her.

She leaned up and there was some part of her that demanded that he kiss her. He couldn't resist. He had to. He tasted her lips, and even though they'd been next to his so recently, he had once again to realize how delicious they were.

He looked up, away from her, and saw Tsali in the kitchen area helping Harry make French toast. The kid was blushing. It's hard to see your father kissing a woman, he realized. He only wished it were harder on the boy to watch his father killing other men. That seemed to be one thing that Tsali had learned to take for granted.

They all sat down when the food was done and ate in near silence, only speaking to ask for butter, syrup, or more milk to drink. Only when the plates had been cleared did Beeker start to talk.

"I don't suppose I even have to take a poll this morning?" He looked around the table and saw that no one was going to surprise him with a sudden desire to avoid action. "Okay. The feds have messed it up again and we've agreed to go in to clean up after them. What do we get?"

The last question was thrown at Delilah. It was spoken with obvious anger and antagonism. No one who had seen it could have guessed that just a short while ago they'd been embracing in a lover's duel on the front steps.

"The general has a significant amount of money stored up, from all accounts. Like many others who're dealing with a warzone enterprise, he's maintained a substantial cash bank of many different currencies. The United States government, I would suppose, doesn't really need to have that back." She said it without any emotion. She wasn't about to take on the Black Berets' leader in one of his moods.

"Yeah, you can buy more land!" Marty piped up, his voice nearly squeaking and undermining his attempt to make the deal attractive to Beeker.

"Just what he needs." Rosie scowled, thinking instead about his years-long battle to get them to buy a nice little condo on some beach with lots of pretty ladies and bars that made funny drinks with paper hats on them.

"Or we can set up a trust fund for Tsali," offered Cowboy in the most overtly manipulative suggestion of all. The kid already had a trust fund that would have done more than get him through college if he wanted—would have bought him a university campus, in fact. That Cowboy would stoop to such a ploy was proof how completely they had all made their decisions to go.

"I suppose you have a plan?" Beeker said, ignoring all their obvious manipulations and returning to Delilah.

"Not really. You're the strategist. I have, though, arranged some raw materials for your use. You can decide just how they're going to be best put into action."

"Oh, you have? And just what is it that you've arranged for us?" Beeker said, an edge of sarcasm in his voice.

5

"Mother of God, will you look at that!" Cowboy was pacing up and down the runway in the Honduran jungle. "How did she do *that?*"

In front of them stood a factory-new helicopter. But not just any bird. It was a Hind-D, the most advanced Eastern Bloc flying machine. "How'd she get this from the Russians?"

"It's actually a Czech model," the well-dressed and obviously discomfited American Air Force officer announced. "It's the armed-assault and antitank version. There are four pods; each one has thirty-two rockets, fifty-seven millimeter. There are four outboard antitank missiles. This baby's armed with the AT-6 type. This could blow away anything in the air or on the ground, just about." The officer looked dismal as he glanced over at the much smaller and less sophisticated Hughes Model 500 Defenders that his Honduran trainees were being stuck with. "I don't know how it was produced."

The officer, a colonel, was in civilian dress. If an American military person had been discovered by Congress this close to the Nicaraguan border, there'd be hell to pay. He wasn't about to make noise about the arrival of this group of ragtag mercs. He was undercover himself enough to know not to ask questions. But the one this flyboy was asking was an awful good one. How *did* someone get a mint-condition, state-of-the-art, fully equipped Czech helicopter to the middle of the Honduran jungle?

"Here's your manual," he said to the flyboy.

"Don't need it," Cowboy announced. "I've flown these—fought against them too."

"This is a model that couldn't possibly have been in service in Nam," the Air Force man stated.

Cowboy looked at him for a moment before he realized that this joker actually thought the only time an American would have flown a combat mission against a Russian-equipped air force was in Indochina. He shrugged. "Like I say, I've flown them before."

Cowboy climbed into the cockpit and played with the switches, familiarizing himself with the wonders of this one piece of equipment that the Russians had made so well. He didn't want to talk to the other man about secret wars in Latin American countries. The asshole thought that his barely camouflaged training assignment here in Honduras was hot shit. Cowboy had been on others.

He was thinking about another copter jockey, one almost as good as he was, who'd flown a Hind-D against him not that many miles from here. That was one of the few times that Cowboy had really admired and really feared another pilot. He had to; the other guy'd come closer than anyone else to sending him on the big one-way ticket off of Earth.

The colonel ignored Cowboy, writing him off as another hotshot. He turned to the one who seemed to be the leader of the group of highly irregular men who'd arrived mysteriously in his training camp. "It doesn't seem right, for you guys to just arrive and take off with a piece of matériel as valuable as this. I think I

43

should have a receipt of some kind, something with your signature on it."

"You're crazy," Beeker said angrily. "You think you're going to get my signature on a piece of paper with ten carbon copies for every office in the Pentagon, you're crazy."

The man walked off. The colonel flushed with anger at the insolence of the guy. It was just that he felt so vulnerable without something to cover his ass. Then he remembered that he himself hadn't officially acknowledged the delivery. He wasn't going to be held responsible by anyone. That gave him some relief. The major lesson they'd taught him at the Air Force Academy had been never to take initiative. He hadn't. There was nothing on paper. Then there was nothing. Life in the modern American fighting forces was just that simple.

He continued on his way, happy now to realize he'd learned his lessons well. That was the problem with the whole world. It let people like this group go about business without paying attention to the really important things that underlined the efficient organization of the American military. Where would this country be without men like the colonel and his old classmate at Colorado Springs, General Cadozza? They were men who'd learned the vital points of strategy and chain of command, not these gung-ho idiots.

He'd made his delivery and he'd done his duty. He wondered, finally, if he should file an incident report, just in case. . . . But, no, he'd been told specifically not to do that. It wasn't his problem anymore.

Beeker stormed away from the career-minded bureaucrat who called himself a soldier and walked across the clearing to the tent where they'd been assigned sleeping space for the short while it would take them to get ready to enter El Salvador under cover.

The camp was one of the many that the government of Honduras allowed to exist here near the point where it, El Salvador, and Nicaragua approached one another. This was a base for the Nicaraguan Contras to come and train, nurse their wounded,

44

pick up their supplies. Theirs was a war that Beeker wouldn't mind getting involved in. But not this time.

It was just a good excuse, perfect cover for them to assemble. No one in this part of the Central American jungle was going to ask too many questions of a group of apparent mercenaries. Anyone who was here to pick up intelligence was doing it for the Sandinistas to the south in Nicaragua. Whatever conclusions they were making would just confuse the enemy in that direction. That made Billy Leaps feel good; it was his little contribution to the Contra effort. He could imagine it now: hundreds of Sandinistas maneuvering to protect a supposedly endangered flank from a phantom attack.

The Black Berets simply weren't going in that direction, though. They were going into El Salvador. It was to the west of here. No one had to know it. Hell, they really didn't have to know if their goddamn escort didn't show up.

Beeker was building up a new head of steam; his anger with the American trainer was cooling and the Salvadoran guide who was supposed to be here was taking the heat instead. He stormed into the tent he had shared with the rest of the Berets last night. "Where the hell . . ."

Beeker let the flap fall back. He froze, not in fear, but in surprise that such a man as this was standing here in front of him.

"This is Lieutenant Amato; Amato, Billy Leaps Beeker, our commander." Harry made the introductions.

The man turned and looked at Beeker. He was the same six feet as the half-breed Cherokee. He had the same constantly tanned complexion. His eyes, though, were a different color. Beeker's were blue, the startling evidence of his father's choice of an Anglo wife. But this man's were brown, almost slanted, in the classical features of a Mayan.

He looks almost like Tsali, Beeker thought. He shouldn't have been surprised, since full-blooded Indians wouldn't be unusual here. The men had grown to think of Tsali's purity as some kind of natural wonder. Of course, Beeker understood

45

that the native-American blood would be more common in Central America.

Why was he so shocked, then? He couldn't find the answer. Then it came to him. He walked to the center of the tent where the cloth ceiling was high enough to allow him to stand up straight. He held out a hand.

The other man took his grasp. "Emanuele Amato, of the Army of the Republic of El Salvador." They shook, coolly and professionally. Because that was what Beeker had seen, what he had responded to. There are some men in the world whose very being announced itself: *warrior*. This Amato was one of them. Before the Spanish conquistadores, before the modern armies, before flying cavalry, Amato's ancestors had been warriors, probably Mayan or one of the other big tribes that had ruled over Central America. Beeker knew it in the deepest parts of his soul. It was the same essence that he had seen in Tsali the first time he had ever laid eyes on the boy who would become his son.

Amato nodded back. Marty and Harry witnessed the whole thing and then turned to one another. It was something they'd seen before and they knew they had no part in it. It was what Marty called "Beeker's Indian thing." That strange communication that Billy Leaps had with other natives of the hemisphere, at least those who were the same kind of man as their leader. They'd learned not to question it, nor try to enter into it.

"What we got here?" Beeker asked the perfunctory question without acknowledging any of the emotions that his team had witnessed. This was his way. You don't tell another man you feel like his brother—and Beeker did instinctively feel that way toward Amato. You simply took it inside and you felt it.

Amato didn't seem to let on for a second that the American half-breed's actions were anything but what he'd expected. He pulled a cloth map from his hip pocket. Paper would have disintegrated in the Central American jungle overnight. The cloth would last at least a week or two. He nodded to the folding

46

table in the center of the tent. Beeker knew what he wanted and quickly cleared its surface.

Amato spread the chart out over the table. "We're here," he pointed to the Honduran base camp. "Your man can fly that thing?"

"Hey, Cowboy could fly your sombrero," Marty chimed in. They all ignored him. Beeker just nodded his assurance to Amato.

"We can leave tomorrow?" It was a question. He was asking Beeker if he'd be ready. Again, Beeker just nodded.

"We will allow the spectators to think we're going into Nicaragua." His finger pointed to the south. "But we'll divert and fly to the Salvadoran border. There's a camp provided for us, but not known to anyone. I sent in a group of scouts and they think it's something for the future, only preparation for another assault next year. There are weapons and explosives stocked, hidden."

"No one on that squad's going to have to be told?" Beeker was immediately ashamed that he'd asked. The man had assured him that the soldier had believed his cover story and he shouldn't have to defend himself. Not a guy like this one. He shook his head, dismissing his own question.

"I'll be with you, your guide." Amato didn't like the sound of his own words and Beeker knew that he'd have to soothe his hurt ego and assure him that he was going to be one of the team. Hopefully the sight of half-Cherokee Beeker would at least tell him that he wasn't going to have to deal with Anglo jerks who expected a Mayan warrior to be no more than a bearer.

"This is almost deserted." Amato's finger swept over a corner of El Salvador, the country's borders clearly demarcated by a bold red line on the map. "The guerillas and the National Guard fought over it so many times a couple years ago that all the civilians fled either to the cities"—Amato's finger moved to the Pacific coastline—"or into Honduras"—now the finger worked its way back to the east.

47

"That's where the fake left-wing group is going to be head-quartered?" Beeker asked with disgust.

Now, for the first time, Amato smiled. "It already is. I got interviewed by the American television the other day as one of the leaders of the feared Chequipac Liberation Front. It was surprisingly easy to talk for them. I started to speak about this war being of no consequence for the real natives of El Salvador, the ancient tribes. By the time I was finished, I sort of liked the sound of it."

Beeker liked that one and nodded. But the intrusion of the American media wasn't something that he really liked at all. Not one bit. "Go ahead, tell us who we're supposed to be. Who are these yo-yos?"

"We're a small tribe, the Chequipac. The story goes that we had been living in almost total seclusion, untouched by modern society. We would have stayed there, a peaceful tribe of hunters and fighters, if the war hadn't intruded on us. But it has. We have, as our symbol, the jaguar. He stays deep in the jungle and avoids humanity, but when humans approach, he kills—quickly and savagely.

"The stories came easily. I remembered them from my grandfather. I'm Chequipac. I've had my peace and quiet in-truded upon. My gods are offended to hell and back. They have been ever since I went to Annapolis."

Beeker studied Amato with a sudden distrust. But it was Marty who spoke first. "Annapolis? Hey, man, were you in the Navy? Huh?"

"No, not the Navy. I was trained by the U.S. Marines."

"Oh, damn," Harry whispered. "I should have known."

6

Cowboy flew the Hind-D perfectly. It was easy to do. The communist helicopter was a dream. He marveled at the power of the machine. The two 2,200 horsepower turboshafts made the thing fly like a bird with its tail on fire.

They weren't as quiet as he'd like; the Russians didn't go in for the little touches like whisperpower, but—damn—they worked. The thing had a range of over 550 miles. This little jaunt was only going to be a hundred, total, and there was a promise of more fuel when they got there. He could have jerked it up to the top speed of over two hundred miles an hour, but there wasn't that much hurry. They'd get there nice and cool and at a hundred and fifty.

Everything would be set up. Everything. Goddamn Beeker, how did he do it? How does it happen? Go to Africa and he finds a jarhead. Go to Asia and he finds a high inside haircut. Fly down to goddamned Central America to rendezvous with some agent of the central government of a country torn apart by a decades-long civil war, and the man who's their key into the whole thing is . . . a *Marine!*

A brown-eyed, slant-faced Marine Indian. He knew that Harry and Marty were just as pissed about it as he was. It was like a curse. *The Curse of the Never-Ending Jarhead!* It had followed them all their life together.

First, in Nam. Cowboy had spent half the war ferrying the idiots in and out. The only difference in the direction they were going was the number of bleeding wounds the Marines had. There was never a slowing down of their enthusiasm, never a hint that they were sorry to be in the jungles of Indochina. No, no, they were happy to be there.

And they always wanted to land in the middle of a firefight; they wanted to take off during an air strike; they wanted to have him wait just a second while they took care of just one more attacking VC. Oh, they'd been pure joy and laughter all the years he'd been there.

It was just like now. He couldn't help but have a little shudder move through his shoulders. There were four men in the craft now. All of them with their shining new rifles. It didn't make any difference that this was a Russkie copter and that their rifles were greasy with Czechoslovakian oil instead of American, that they were called AK-47's instead of M-16's. It was all the same to them.

The jungle helped make it seem that way. El Salvador was as green, as hilly, as hot, as humid, as treacherous, as Nam had been. It was all an instant reply of a movie that Cowboy had never wanted to see again.

The fact that the names had changed didn't matter a whole lot to him. The droning of the engines made this too real. The landscape did too. All of it too real.

They were approaching their destination. Cowboy could see the well-prepared landing zone. Just like so many others in his life. It had been recently cleared, and it had to have been. This was a living beast, this kind of jungle. It would move in on you in nothing flat. Only a few months and the whole thing would be given back to mother nature.

The Hind-D seemed to lower itself gently. He forgot his worries as he sensed the enormous command he had of the bird. This was his joy.

But once the copter was on the ground and he had cut the engines his sense of power was over. Cowboy climbed out of the craft and hit the ground, no longer the pilot, just another guy now. He stretched, his arms upraised and his belly distended as he exaggerated his need to get some blood pulsing through his body.

Then the mortars began.

BAM! To the right.

KAPLOOOOOOOOP! To the left.

He collapsed into a ball and rolled away from the helicopter. The damn thing had more than three quarters of a tank of fuel in it. A direct hit and they were *gone!*

Then the two of them—Beeker and Amato—were racing over him. Their AK-47's were on automatic and they were sweeping the edge of the clearing. They moved like panthers into the brush, pushing it aside with their elbows, somehow managing to keep the big guns moving and firing, the rat-a-tat-a-tat-tat of the Russian assault weapons exploding the silence of the jungle, sending flocks of multicolored birds into the sky screeching, but not loudly enough to hide the sound of the continuing gunfire.

Harry and Marty didn't need to be told what to do. They raced into the jungle, each one far to either side of the two point men. Their own rifles were ready, willing, and able. There was no question about that.

Cowboy stayed frozen, unarmed but for a revolver in his pocket. He was exposed and scared, honest to God scared.

Suddenly, Beeker was backing out of the green wall; he was crouching down to the right. Cowboy took cover and watched, and knew that whatever was causing the Beak to do that, it meant trouble. Billy Leaps didn't run from a battle. He didn't know the meaning of the word *retreat*. The only possibility was that he was setting a trap of some kind.

Then it happened. Three men crashed through the brush barrier into the clearing. They had rifles in their hands. As soon as they got into the open area they turned and lifted them into firing position.

Except that Billy Leaps Beeker was there. He was holding his nice new Kalishnikov at his hip. He was smiling. He only had the slightest moment to smile, but he did. Cowboy saw it, as he had often before. Then Beeker, unseen by the enemy, opened up.

The line of automatically propelled bullets was visible. It began with the poor bugger on the left. He got it first. He caught it in a clean line right at the waist.

But his friends didn't notice it in time. They didn't have a chance. Maybe they weren't surprised by the sound of the rifle. Maybe it was because they were expecting something like it, thinking it was just their comrade starting too soon. Maybe they just didn't have time. The line of fire moved to the second man. He'd been in the middle. This time the multiple bullets cut through the man's chest.

Beeker seemed to have mastered the Russian rifle's aim to his satisfaction. He didn't seem to think he needed the automatic anymore. The third man got his calling card with a single bullet —right in the middle of his skull.

It was right then and right there that Cowboy remembered why he'd made it out of Southeast Asia alive. Sure, the Marines were forever getting him into ridiculous situations, but they also had the knack of getting him out of them alive.

Beeker rushed back into the thick undergrowth of jungle that surrounded the landing zone. The rest were still hidden by the green and seemingly impenetrable wall of the forest.

Somebody sure as hell found something. There was a sudden and ferocious exchange of fire. Cowboy felt that sweat of battle running down his neck. It was the sour one, the one that made everything so damn tense, nervous. There was something going on in that greenness. It had to do with death and dying, it had to do with the enemy being offed or the enemy being victorious. As much as he knew that all of the guys were totally trained and as much as he utterly trusted them, Cowboy couldn't help the feelings of dread and suspicion that were coming over him now.

Yes, they were the best. But there were some other good ones out there. Someday he'd be standing in a place like this and when it was over, he wouldn't be one of the ones on the winning team. Someday. He hoped it wasn't today.

Cowboy held his pistol tightly. This was a scenario that they'd played too often in their practice. His duty was to guard the copter, to make sure that there wasn't a hotshot in there who might want to make a hero out of himself by trying to take the unguarded craft. The pistol felt like a toy in Cowboy's hand, but it was all he had. For once he actually missed Marty Appelbaum. The guy was an asshole, but if Marty was here there'd be plenty of firepower, it came with the package.

In about five minutes the four men returned. Beeker just nodded to Cowboy. Marty had to crow a bit. "Nothing left there, we got all of them. Not a living soul left. Got their mortars too."

"They'll come in handy," Beeker admitted.

He and Amato went over to the dead bodies. There were only two of them here in sight, but there were probably more back where the men had come from. Amato crouched down, a scowl on his face. "National Guard."

"Your guys, huh!" Marty rubbed it in. "These were the ones that we were supposed to trust so much. Hell, you had them set up the base—"

"Not mine!" Amato insisted angrily. "These are a special unit." He looked at Beeker. "These are Cadozza's men."

"How do you know that? Tell me how you know that!" Marty wasn't going to give up his irritating questions now.

But Beeker didn't ask. Again, the half-breed just nodded. He knelt down on the floor of the clearing beside Amato and rifled through the pockets of one of the dead men. There was nothing. No identification of any kind. He looked at the rest of them. They understood: a soldier should have some kind of ID on him. To go into the field without it meant that something was up, and that something was probably not legit. They should know. They'd done it in Nam.

"Guess it's time for us to do some talking," Beeker said calmly to Amato. "Let's get rid of these bodies, make up a camp, get a pot of coffee on. Then we'll get some info from you."

Amato agreed and the whole group went to work.

"A war goes on as long as our civil war and the lines get broken down. The reasons why people are on what side get lost. Good guys, bad guys—your funny television people always try to make it out that way. But in a long war it just isn't what goes on."

The Salvadoran was sipping the harsh and bitter coffee he'd made himself. It was stronger tasting and much more potent than the consumer specials the Americans were used to. But they weren't paying much attention to the taste. They wanted to know what this man they were going to have to rely on had to say.

"We have a chance to establish a real democracy here in this country now. The central government's finally strong enough and the communists are losing on most fronts. But it's gone on for so long—this fighting—that there are splinter groups all over the place. This isn't left wing versus right wing. This isn't anything like that. There are those two, the central government, and the communists in the mountains, but in between there are plenty of others.

"Anyone with enough money to hire an army of his own has a claim to being kind of a warlord here. The government just isn't strong enough yet to divert any of its resources to anything but the war with the communists.

"Cadozza is one of many of the warlords, but not the only

54

one, just the strongest one. He plays it much cooler than the rest, insisting that he's really a good guy, on the right side. He's just an ultraconservative, he says. But his politics aren't the kind that take place in a legislature. They're the kind that you vote with bullets."

"That's right!" Marty said belligerently. He looked at Beeker. "I told Del that Cadozza was an okay dude, he speaks our language."

Beeker stared at Appelbaum for a moment, but Harry kept everything calm. "No, Marty, this time he's on the wrong side."

"Damn," Marty muttered, "I don't get it."

Amato waited to make sure that this was sufficient to take care of the strange blond man's opinions. It obviously was, since no one was even paying attention to him anymore.

"Cadozza's the type who not only wants to get rid of the communists in the mountains, he wants to get rid of anyone in those cities that the government rules who might want to question his activities. There are members of the guard who are blindly loyal to him, so loyal that they take orders only from him.

"There was a time when they weren't even in the guard. They were just bands of hired hands. But the government had to make peace with the right wing, and Cadozza's men were a part of the deal. We took them in." Amato obviously didn't like the memory of the compromise.

"They still respond to his special orders. They're a hit squad, ready to take out his political opponents when it's necessary. Those—and anyone who might interfere with his business interests."

Beeker thought for a moment. "And as the government makes it easier for him to control the politics, his men can be taking on those special assignments more and more often."

"You got it," Amato agreed. "Thing is, it seems that Cadozza's other interests are getting so big and lucrative, he might just be getting together enough money to take over the country anyhow. Word has it that he doesn't have much of a taste for politics anymore."

"We'll just have to see that he loses his other tastes too," the leader of the Black Berets announced.

7

There were some tastes that Rosie never had any intention of losing. Many of them were right here in the presidential suite of the finest hotel in El Paso. This made sense to him. This made great sense to him.

Outside his window he could see the slow-moving expanse of the Rio Grande. On the other side was Ciudad Juárez, El Paso's twin city, or so they called it. The two places had little in common.

El Paso was booming and glittering and moving with all the pizzazz of American gusto. It had high-rise buildings like this one, wide streets, good schools, and a state university that made lots of national championship tournaments. It had big shiny cars wheeling down its freeways and it had fancy clothes in its department-store windows.

Ciudad Juárez had only one big thing to match it all—it had a few hundred thousand people who wanted to walk across that river and live in El Paso to escape the grimness, the poverty, and the filth you have to suffer if you don't live in the United States of America.

Rosie thought about all those folks and he honestly did feel badly for them. It was a real shame and he didn't mean to deny it. But, then, he was living here and he had a role to perform and it was a lovely one, because it meant that he not only was on the right side of the river, he was about fifteen floors above it in a suite that came with a big king-sized bed, a bathroom bigger than some of those houses over there in Mexico, and a living room that his momma would have loved to see.

Right now there wasn't anyone but Rosie in it. A shame, he thought, a real shame. All this luxury wasted on a big black man like him. He'd just have to change that.

He looked at his watch and saw that it was after seven. There were some places he was supposed to check out. He could try them now, at the dinner hour.

Rosie was dressed in one of his ghetto uniforms. He loved it, it made him laugh whenever this kind of stuff happened. The Berets had their own rags, things that Beeker had had made up when they had first gotten back together again. When they put on those camouflaged uniforms it seemed that they were . . . changed. Something happened when a soldier put on his uniform. Something very deep.

The others, the ones who had gone down to El Salvador, probably knew about that right now. They probably had on the clothing that they would need in order to move through the jungle, the cotton that would absorb perspiration, the boots that wouldn't rot in the tropical climate, the grease they'd have to put on their faces to make sure they were hidden in the darkness of the rain forest.

Rosie had a different assignment from theirs, and that meant he had to be wearing a different uniform. That was all. He strode out of his suite and down the corridor to the elevator. A married middle-aged couple came out of their own room and moved toward him. As soon as they could register their shock on their faces, Rosie knew that he was wearing just the right thing.

Poor souls. It must be hard on them to see this big black man wearing a sharkskin suit so shiny that the thread seemed to be fluorescent. He had on his *mean* shades, the ones with lenses so dark there was no way to see behind them; wearing them indoors made him look all the more ominous. He had a hat on his head as well. A fine hat. He just couldn't resist proving to this nice little white couple that he was their worst dream come true.

Acting as though he just wanted to be polite to the lady, Rosie lifted the hat off. Underneath it his skull was shaven. It completed the image for the two of them, totally.

They'd never understand that it was the completion of Rosie's image for himself as well. He'd made Beeker shave his head just before they'd all split up in Shreveport. It was Rosie's own ritual. To go into battle a man shaved his head as a part of his preparation. And whatever else, Rosie's assignment in El Paso was as much a battle as anything the rest of them might experience.

The woman couldn't control herself, and put a hand to her mouth in shock. Rosie just ignored her bad manners and smiled at her. It was a nice vote of confidence, actually. It'd been a while since Rosie had put on this particular act himself, and he liked knowing that it was still working.

When the elevator opened, he stood aside with a grand gesture to allow the couple to enter first. They did, a little bit too slowly. Then Rosie entered the cage and pressed the button for the lobby. He began to whistle a tune, a happy one, one you'd expect a black gangster to know.

Rosie was done having his fun with the folks. He let them be after the elevator had deposited all of them in the lobby. He strode directly out through the front doors and hailed a cab. The next car in line pulled up. The hotel lackey gratefully accepted Rosie's tip while he held the door open for him.

"Where to, bro'?" the black cabdriver asked.

"You know where the Boston Club is?" Rosie asked, pulling out an enormous cigar and biting off its tip.

The driver only whistled. He wasn't surprised, he was just appropriately impressed. "Course I do." Then he pulled away.

Rosie leaned back in the seat and watched the city's neighborhoods fly past him. Soon the taxi was entering the black area. Rosie could have smelled it. It could be here in Texas; it could be in New Hampshire. It didn't make a difference. There was always one and it was always the same.

And in the middle of it there was always a Boston Club.

The building wasn't all that noticeable. It looked like many others nearby. Newly constructed and done without a lot of concern for any good looks. It seemed just to be a functional affair. But as soon as Rosie had walked past the front door and into the cocktail area, he knew he had made the right choice.

The place was as ostentatious and overly decorated as it could be, all full of fake red velvet on the concrete walls and thick-pile wall-to-wall rugs on the floors. The tables were banquettes lined against the wall, each one covered with an impossibly colored Naugahyde. There was soft music in the background, soul transformed into Muzak. This was where the rich blacks came. There was no doubt about it.

He let the foxy-looking hostess take him to a good table. Part of this whole thing was to make an impression; he overtipped her, as he had been overtipping every black server he'd come in contact with since arriving in El Paso. She'd remember him; that's what he wanted her to do.

He ordered a double Black Label on the rocks and sent the woman on her way. He still had a lot of his cigar left. He sat back and fired it up while he took in the room.

It was early for the Boston Club. But it was going. This was the place, probably the one and only good restaurant in the ghetto by most standards—Rosie had his own and would have preferred a meal made up of good, down-home soul food. But this was the place to drink expensive Scotch and to eat beef.

60

More important, this was the place to come to prove to other blacks in El Paso that you could *afford* to do it.

Rosie waited for the hostess to bring him his order. When she returned, she smiled, not talking while she put the thick glass of iced amber liquor down in front of him.

"Had a chance to look at the menu yet?" she asked.

Rosie didn't try to hide the way he was studying her. He let his eyes roam up and down her figure. It wasn't hard to do, not with the invitation that the clinging crêpe dress offered him. It also made it easy for him to really study what he saw. There was nothing under that dress. Nothing at all.

Her skin was a light cocoa, one of Rosie's favorites. Her hair was carefully combed in a tightly held Afro. The top of her dress dived down into her cleavage. There was so much bare space there that he could see that those breasts were just as firm as possible. The fabric was so thin that he could even make out the round circle of her nipples. They looked like the kind of dinner that he wouldn't mind having right now.

Waitresses hear every line in the book. They are the kind of women that you simply cannot impress with a new attempt at humor. Marty was the type who was always trying to make it with these working women. He never succeeded because he was always making a fool of himself, telling them that they were the midnight special that he wanted to put on his blue plate or some such other idiocy.

Rosie knew better. He just looked. He looked again and he made sure that the movements of his head left nothing to this beautiful woman's imagination.

Finally he said, "No. Why don't you just tell me what's good to eat here."

She looked at him suspiciously, waiting for him to make his innuendo more obvious. But he just sat there with that smirk. "Place is famous for its ribs and chicken plate. There's the surf and turf special—lobster tail. South African lobster tail."

"Girl, I wouldn't eat any tail from that place. Come on, tell me what's good."

"Steak. The bigger, the better. It's Texas, remember?"

"The biggest, then. Rare. Rare so the blood oozes out of it and makes a little puddle on my plate." Rosie smiled more broadly. "I like a little blood there, makes my potatoes real tasty. You better throw on an extra potato, while you're at it. And you can bring me a salad with that Roquefort dressing. Got me a hunger tonight."

She looked, no friendliness on her face. "Haven't seen you here."

"From out of town," Rosie answered easily.

She picked up the menu but didn't move. "You looking for something in particular here in El Paso?"

Rosie understood immediately that this was his chance. It was simply coming earlier than he had expected. "Got to find some people to do business with, that's all."

"I thought that might be it." She didn't say more, but moved away.

Now, that was very interesting, Rosie thought. Very interesting indeed. He watched the setup here in the Boston Club even more carefully. He wanted to see the way the girl handled the information that he had just given her. Someplace else it might have seemed like the banter of any traveling businessman and a waitress, but Rosie knew there had been more going on here.

The woman didn't seem to stop her work. That was surprising. She should have assigned one of the regular waitresses to his table, but didn't. She should have had to tell someone what she'd learned, but instead she just went on with her duties.

It didn't take her long to come up with Rosie's salad. The bright-green leaves of lettuce were topped with tomatoes that were fresh from some nearby farm. The dressing was a thick creamy glop with clumps of the blue-veined cheese obvious to his eye.

Rosie would wait. He was used to it. Waiting was part of the job. In the meantime he would enjoy his meal. He let the girl take the bowl when he was finished. Almost immediately she brought out a platter with an enormous slab of beef flanked by two large baked potatoes. All of it was sitting in a pool of warm juices, the blood that would congeal if he allowed it to cool.

Rosie had no intention of doing that, and went right for the food. He sawed at the steak, dug into the potatoes, and soaked up the liquids with them. He could always use a good meal, God knows that'd always been true. He had no need to display good manners right now. His healthy appetite was as appropriate as any other trait for what he was doing.

There was a commotion on the other side of the dining room. Rosie looked up, irritated at whoever was disturbing his meal.

"Fuckin' bitch!" a tall black man with straightened and greased hair screamed. He was standing, or trying to—the table he was sitting at with three women was pressed against the wall and he couldn't seem to manage to get his hips up enough. Then, he lunged for the girl he'd screamed at.

When he did, the table went flying and dishes, glasses, and silverware clattered on the floor. The three women had been trying to keep their cool; Rosie hadn't heard them raise their voices before. But now they screamed.

This was just too annoying. Rosie stood up and stormed over to the fracas. By now the man had one of the women by her hair, the one he'd been angry at. She was young, she was attractive, and Rosie saw no good reason why this dummy should be hurting her, none at all.

Rosie reached over and grabbed the guy by the collar of his shirt, pulling him back with one violent motion that surprised him so much, he released the girl. She yelped and drew back, pressing herself against the seat.

"What you want to make my dinner so unpleasant for, fool?" Rosie asked the man.

The other guy had a ridiculous look about him. Rosie had thought his own appearance was amusing, but this man was in it for real. His hair was so thick with oil that it had crusted. He had a moustache that was no wider than a pencil point. There were dozens of thin gold chains around his neck.

"Let me go, nigger" was all the reply Rosie got. He didn't

think it a very pleasant way for one man to greet another, and he responded by sending a fist pounding into the soft gut of the man.

Rosie thrust out his arm, afraid the man was going to upchuck—and if he was, Rosie didn't want to ruin his fine suit.

Rosie threw his arm out straight and the man collapsed back onto his seat. The women were paralyzed both by the fear of this man that had gripped them earlier, and now by the sight of the black monster who was hovering over them. Rosie went to say something nice to them, calm them down, when he felt the unmistakable pressure of a pistol barrel in his side.

"Don't move."

The voice was female, soft and alluring, even if it was standing behind the metal of a gun. Rosie followed the direction, quickly taking in the situation. He allowed only his head to rotate, slowly.

There was the woman who'd served him. He looked down. He recognized the Walther PPK/S .380 held firmly in her grip. "Where'd you get a Kraut gun?" He smiled at her.

"My daddy," she replied. She turned to the woman who had been the target of the man's anger. "Maria, you take Stick out of here; get him home. You tell him to call me tomorrow morning. Don't worry, you don't have to say anything to him. You just tell him that Jez wants to speak to him. Now, go on, get out while I deal with our new friend here."

The three women moved quickly, obviously impressed with the authority of the gunwoman. Rosie understood that her authority wasn't just coming from her pistol.

Rosie stood there, his hands automatically up and away from his body in a show of deference, and waited while the three women dragged the still coughing man up onto his feet and half led, half carried him through the front bar area of the restaurant and out onto the street.

"Fine group of people you have coming here," he finally said.

"Seems you're just like the rest of them," the woman snorted.

"Oh, believe me, baby, I'm different as they come." Rosie

gave her his broadest smile, the one with a big flash of teeth, and calmly lowered his arms. "Mind if I go back to my dinner now?"

The woman lowered the pistol and stared at him. "Think I might even join you."

"I thought you might want to." Rosie walked over to his table. He noticed that the other patrons had gone back to their meals. The excitement hadn't upset them. It proved his suspicion that they were used to little scenes like that in the Boston Club.

Rosie was already chewing on another piece of his steak by the time the woman sat down. He'd watched her speaking to another of the girls, obviously getting her duties reassigned. "If you're going to sit with me, might as well tell me what your name is," he said between enormous bites.

"Jezebel Strauss." She had brought back a drink and took a healthy swipe at it now.

"Strauss, and you said your daddy gave you that gun?"

"German. He was a German. Momma met him when she was stationed in Germany. He was a good man. I loved him a lot. He's the one taught me to shoot a gun. He didn't think it made any difference to a bullet if it was a female at the other end of it. It killed just the same. I was his only child, so I got all his love, all his teaching. You name it, guns, money . . ."

". . . Sex," Rosie finished for her, and chewed still another bite of steak. He studied her reaction to his challenge. He saw a flush of anger and guilt come over her. Yeah, he was right, Jezebel got a lot of stuff from her daddy, all right.

"That's none of your business. My business is you busting up my restaurant."

"Yours, huh?" That explained a lot of it.

"I've owned the Boston Club since the day it opened." Jez was obviously proud of it; it was her accomplishment.

"Quite a place," Rosie said, wiping his mouth. His plate was clean. "Takes quite a woman to run a place that all the whores and pimps of a city spend their time in."

She wasn't surprised or offended by his remark. She just shrugged. "They got good money."

"Lots of people got good money." He spoke the words with as much meaning as he could.

"Tell me about yours."

"You'd need a whole lot of time to hear about that."

She smiled and finished off her drink. "Let's you and me go upstairs, to my apartment. I got some awful good cognac there, for special guests."

My, my, Rosie thought as he looked around the room. It was grand, as ostentatious as the restaurant downstairs, but it was a girl's dream come true. Every little frilly thing that she could ever have wanted was right here, he was sure of it.

The walls were painted in various shades of pink. The curtains were white, lined with frilly lace. The carpet was an exaggerated white pile. The furniture was set up in a block of connecting seats that left it a square with three sides of bolsters, and the center all filled in with Ottoman-like cushions that made it seem like a huge bed.

Rosie was sitting on the edge of it, watching Jez pour them brandy. He was studying her ass. It was fine, just fine, the kind he liked, high and firm with that special appearance that only black women seem to be able to inherit. There was none of that overly soft ass that other women seem to have.

Rosie felt himself getting hard just at the thought of touching Jez there. He was going to do it, he knew that. It was a part of his assignment. *Too bad,* he thought, *that I have to go through such terrible torture for the sake of the assignment.*

She turned. He'd admired her tits before, but now he was falling in love with them. The difference was they were something to look at in the restaurant, here they were something to use. He was going to love using them, so big, their ends pointing up in the air with youth and insolence.

Jez brought the big snifters over and handed one to him before she sat down on the next cushion. He could see from her eyes that she knew they were going to fuck. There was that special combination of fear and anticipation that came over a woman when she was with Rosie and knew it was going to happen. No matter how many times he told them, they just couldn't believe they weren't going to be hurt. It was his size, he guessed, and the way his body gave them hope and dread that his size was going to be matched in that special part of himself that was covered right now and giving him so much trouble as it struggled to get free of the newly created tightness in his pants.

But you just don't come on to a girl this quick. You let her build up to it, you give her a chance to prepare herself. He used the silent moments to think about Jez. She was about thirty. It was a good age, the one at which a female thinks she might be losing her attractiveness and is willing to give herself away easily, anxious for the proof that she can still get herself a man.

It was also good because it was an age at which a female had enough experience to be able to do it really well. Really well.

That thought was too much for Rosie. A smile had crept over his face and he turned it to her now. She was ready, there was a little movement, her tongue came out to wet her lips. She shifted on the cushion so her nipples were pointed directly at him. Rosie reached out a single palm and put it on her shoulder. He pressed down, ever so slightly, as though he were testing her.

If he was, she passed with flying colors. As soon as she felt that pressure, she managed to put the cognac snifter on the floor and then fluidly reclined her body on the big couch. Rosie put his own glass down and then sprawled out next to her.

She moved over to him, placing her legs and her hips up against his. Her eyes were closed. She was telling him to do what he wanted, she was waiting. She wouldn't have to do that for long.

Rosie snaked a hand up under her skirt. There weren't any panties there. He rubbed softly and was immediately rewarded with a soft moan of joy.

The woman had given him one good meal already, Rosie realized, and there was no reason for him not getting another.

He went through the motions, playing with her breasts with one hand, manipulating her sex with the other, getting her hotter and hotter, making her think that her pleasures had been paid attention to. If you go too fast, he knew, the women just thought you were forgetting them. Rosie never forgot women. How could a man do that?

When he'd finished with the formalities, he got down to what he wanted to do. Her dress came off quickly and easily with her willing help. She was naked now, her body just as stunning as he had expected it to be, the cocoa color all over her skin, darker in some places, but that only made it more appealing to him.

Rosie spread her legs. She was compliant, only moaning in anticipation. But she wasn't ready for what came next. Rosie moved onto his back and then, with one of his huge arms, he dragged her over on top of him. She was forced to straddle his stomach.

Now his hands took her waist. He lifted again, bringing her up, bringing all that naked, good-looking, good-smelling flesh right up his body; her legs were against his chest, then his neck, and then it was right where he wanted it.

He was so into it that he barely could hear her moans as they climbed up and up, driving themselves into near screams of pleasure. Then he could feel her tensing. She was trying to escape now. It was typical, she was afraid it was going to be over too soon. Silly women, it was just the first course. They never understood that this was all just hors d'oeuvres.

Her body began to spasm. He slowed a bit, letting her noises subside, letting her calm herself. In a bit he thought she had.

That was when he calmly rolled her off him. She was spread out over the cushions. There was a gaze on her face as she studied him with an almost wistful look. Rosie stood up and smiled down at her.

Now he finally took off his shirt, exposing his massive chest.

He kicked off his shoes. Then he undid his belt and unzipped his pants. He tore off his slacks and his underwear at the same time.

He climbed onto the cushions between her legs and was moving carefully, lovingly, until he heard another little cry from her: "Oh, yes. . . ."

8

"Are you really leaving?" Here the woman was on her own, had her own restaurant—and from the way she'd handled that pimp she had to have some other things going as well—and she was just like any other female in the world, just about. She wanted to know the man she'd just given it to would remember her.

"Don't you worry, baby," Rosie said, bending down to give her cheek one last peck. "We're going to have lunch tomorrow. You be ready for me about noon."

"Okay." Jezebel moved under the sheet.

Rosie was finished dressing. He waved his way out of the owner's apartment over the restaurant and moved down the stairway to the first floor.

Business had picked up again. The true colors of the Boston Club were showing themselves. The diners were all gone, there were just the drinkers and the dealers, the talkers and the people on the prowl for sex—selling or buying, there wasn't going to be much given away in this place at this time of night.

The air was gathering cigarette smoke. The music was turned up and it wasn't the canned stuff that they had for the eating crowd, it was more raucous. There was a small area cleared for dancing and there were a few couples swaying to the sounds. At least one of the women—a white woman—was out of it. Not just drunk, Rosie could tell that. She was on something very heavy.

This wasn't the time for him to deal with it. Rosie was going after more than a little drug user. He walked through the bar area, and was ready to push open the door to the street when an arm came out and stopped him.

"Been waiting for you." Rosie saw a man with a Colt .45 in his hand, a hand that was only partly concealed beneath his suit jacket. It was Stick, the pimp he'd roughed up earlier.

"I don't go for drag queens," Rosie said smugly, pulling his arm free.

The insult stunned Stick more than a fist would have. Rosie was ready to walk away but he found his exit blocked by still another piece of metal. This one was a knife, a very large knife with a glistening edge.

There was no indication that anyone was paying any attention to what was going on. There sure as hell wasn't any hint that anyone was planning on coming to Rosie's rescue. He took in the situation. There were two of them, both armed, and they might have friends. That was just a chance that Rosie would have to take. "Guess we should be willing to do a little negotiation around here."

"Let's do that. In the parking lot," the one with the knife said. Rosie could tell the man knew how to use his weapon. It wasn't just the practiced way he held it. It was also the long scar across the entire left side of his face. If a man got a cut like that and still came back after someone, with the fight still in him, he was no amateur. He could be a fool, but he certainly knew what was going on.

Rosie decided not to argue. His agreement gave Stick a little more confidence. He used the tip of the barrel to push Rosie.

That was too bad; that was something that Rosie wouldn't forget.

The scar-faced man made his own mistake. He turned his back on Rosie. He was the only one that Rosie had any respect for. And he had to go and make a stupid move like that. Rosie thought it was just too bad. Here the man was trusting his pal with the Colt and he should really know better.

As soon as the knifeman had his free hand on the door handle, Rosie made his move. He threw an elbow backward so hard that there was an immediate whoosh of air from the man's lungs.

There was that Colt back there somewhere, but Rosie knew the knife in front of him had to be taken care of. That was the real danger in this fight. Rosie grabbed both the upper arms of the man and pulled him harshly backward. The man was only momentarily surprised. He had damn good instincts. As soon as he felt his balance going, he corrected for it. Rosie was impressed.

But the man couldn't do everything. There he was, holding on to his knife, trying to get a firm footing, and he couldn't do it all, especially not while Rosie was throwing him around in a circle that quickly had him facing the opposite direction, right into the barrel of Stick's Colt. It happened just in time for both of them to see the gun go off.

The loud CRACK reverberated through the dining room. The crowd reacted instantly. They were practiced in this; most of them dived under the tables, knowing that an attempt to run for the doors would be their worst error, leaving them exposed to any more fire that could take place.

Stick was shocked. His face froze. Something had gone very wrong and it was more than just missing Rosie. He'd killed the wrong man.

Rosie didn't give him time to think about it. He quickly threw the dying body in front of him, right at Stick, who staggered when the body struck—not just from the force of the blow, but from the very idea that it had happened.

72

He certainly didn't have time to wonder why Rosie was ducking down quickly, and he didn't have time to react to Rosie's quick move toward him. The knife had fallen and clattered on the linoleum doorstop of the restaurant. Rosie had it in his hand now, the reason for his quick maneuver. It was still in his hand when it cut right into Stick's stomach.

Rosie made sure that the one thrust went right to the handle. He didn't do anything else until he could feel that cloth of the man's shirt. Then he ripped upward with one powerful stroke.

Stick fell to the floor in a heap. Somewhere in the room a woman screamed. Someone hit her. There were dozens of eyes fixed on him. Rosie still had the bloody knife in his hand. They were waiting to see what he was going to do with it. The place was used to violence, all right. There was no question about that.

Rosie went over to the bar and spoke to the man behind it. "I guess you better tell Jezebel to get down here. She's going to have to miss her beauty rest tonight."

"No cops at all, huh?" Rosie said as he watched Jezebel directing the cleanup. "You got a few dozen witnesses to two deaths and you aren't going to call the police?" It was clear from his voice that he thought it was funny. It certainly wasn't bothering him. He just sat at the stool and sipped at the Johnnie Walker Black Label that he was holding.

At first, she seemed to ignore him, intent instead on the progress that the cleaning people were making on removing the mess that had once been a part of Stick's body. But then she turned to face him. "What are the police going to do about the death of a second-rate pimp and a hit man with a sheet as long as your arm?"

He liked her honesty. Shrugging, he asked, "So what happens?"

"What do you care, so long as there's nothing else going to happen?"

"But something else does have to happen, woman. You can't

73

tell me that there was no one out there that cared about the man. Someone is going to react."

"Everything's taken care of all right." That was all she would say, and that interested Rosie very much.

"What's going to happen to his women?"

She looked over at him. "You want them?"

"They yours to give?"

She nodded.

Rosie smiled. "I don't need any more women than I got. But I think you and me have a lot to talk about."

She shrugged and led him to one of the back booths. When they were seated she ordered a bourbon-and-ginger for herself and another Scotch for Rosie.

"Look, you're good in bed, you're very good in bed. I liked it. I hope we'll do it again. But you got something else you want, from me, from El Paso. I'm tired of the games, get straight with me. What's going on?"

Rosie knew he was on delicate ground. He had to patch over the personal stuff first. "I didn't know that you were going to be the person I would have to deal with here. I just saw me a nice-looking woman working hard for her money, that was all. You got to know that before I say anything more."

The drinks arrived. Jez took a drink of hers before she answered him. "That whole scene with you was a nice fantasy. I don't get men like that—ever. I get men. But not like that. Usually they work for me, they know me and want something from me. There are more than enough of those, believe me. But I usually never . . . fraternize with the customers."

"Sure sounds like a military word to me."

Jez hesitated. "I told you my mother was stationed in Germany when she met my father. She was a nurse in the Air Force. Fell in love with a big blond man that never would have looked at her black ass back home and married him. She got canned 'cause of it. But there were no regrets. Daddy did all right by her."

"Daddy still alive?" Rosie pressed.

"Daddy died; so did Momma."

"You do all this with their money?"

"It was theirs. There was more than cash. You put my momma's connections together with my daddy's, and you get them mixed up together, you get some very interesting results. You get a very good business."

"Now, that's what we got to talk about. See, I came down here knowing damn well that El Paso has many charms, but the most wonderful is being just right across the border from Mexico. I just know that makes for some very interesting import/export possibilities. I just know it. I only have to figure out how to arrange to meet a supplier."

"You met the biggest supplier in El Paso tonight, me."

"Not girls."

"Hell, no." Jez was angry at the implication. "I just let a couple guys like Stick have their good time here. It's part of the business. I get a little cut, it's important."

"Keeps them in line?"

"Keeps them in their place. Just what are you asking all these questions for?"

"Well"—Rosie played his role now—"seems I got a sugar distribution business in Buffalo, New York. Seems I used to import my goods from certain places. Seems my suppliers are having a lot of trouble replacing their own sources and my customers are very upset. I got to find some sugar for them."

It was a barely hidden code. He needed a new source for some hard street drugs. He was a big-time dealer who had been cut off somehow. But if Jezebel wanted to ignore him, she could. She chose to take the bait instead. "There's only one place to buy sugar nowadays. Seems the government import quotas have shut everyone else down."

"Can you put me in touch with this outfit that still has a quota to fill?"

"I can," Jez said, sipping her drink again. "If you know how to speak Spanish."

9

Beeker looked around the compound they had set up. It was familiar. It would have been familiar in the middle of the Arctic or in the middle of a desert. He'd seen it, in one form or another, a hundred times.

It was an armed camp, better protected than most. What they had originally seen as a landing zone was now carefully marked out with single-man tents lined up along one side. Marty had placed in a straight line the mortars that they'd captured, but each one was pointed in a different direction. They could be quickly used to repulse an assault from east, west, north, or south. But now there was less chance of a surprise attack, at any rate.

They had worked hard to clear the forest even farther back than it had been. Beyond that, they had at least thinned it out. There were good sight lines for a couple hundred feet.

The camp was on the top of a mountain. From where he stood Beeker had a clear view of the torturous Salvadoran terrain. No wonder the civil war had gone on for so long. This was cruel country, the kind that could hide a small guerrilla force easily. It was also the kind that made anything close to traditional warfare impossible.

Tanks would be a waste. Troop carriers couldn't possibly make it through the rough paths that were the only roads. Helicopters were the only form of modern equipment that could be used here. Lots and lots of the birds to fly men and materiel in and out, to do the necessary recon. And there would be many, many times when a commander would want the firepower of the copters to act as his major assault weapon.

Now he knew why Delilah had arranged for the Hind-D. Cowboy was really going to earn his keep on this trip. There was the undeniable advantage of the presence of the communist helicopter for later propaganda uses. But for right now the big machine was the thing they had that no one else in this country could match.

He looked back at the Hind-D that was still sitting in the middle of the cleared area. He thought the bastard was ugly. He thought all the helicopters in the world were ugly. Their huge roters and their ungraceful lines made it appear impossible that all that misshapen lump of metal could really fly.

Cowboy was already at it. He was hard at work doing maintenance. If Beeker would let him, the flier would be happy to polish it inch by inch with a toothbrush. Whatever Beeker might think of helicopters, Cowboy loved them to death—usually someone else's death.

Amato walked up to him now. The Salvadoran had been withdrawn. Maybe it was his character, but Beeker was sure not. He was positive it was Amato's ongoing embarrassment that he had been betrayed.

"This place is very close to Cadozza's headquarters," Amato said. He presented it matter-of-factly. But he was presenting more than information. He was explaining why his troops' movement could have been detected when they did the original work on the clearing.

Beeker didn't respond. He accepted the explanation.

"What else do you know of his activities?" Beeker finally asked. It was time to make sure he and Amato were dealing from the same deck.

The Salvadoran looked out over the expanse of mountains. "I told you about his right-wing activities here. His hit squads are the worst kinds of vigilantes. They attack anyone who in any way interferes with what he wants to have happen. The press, the legitimate opposition, all of them are possible targets for him. *The Lion of Salvador.*" Amato spoke the nickname with full contempt.

"He gets his money from the U.S. The conservative groups up there, the armchair mercenaries who want to feel a part of the action, they all donate to him. That, and the big thing. The drugs.

"I know a little bit about how you got involved. I know that your purpose here is to stop Cadozza's drug traffic. It moves through here, some of it, but most of it, from what we can tell, goes through other countries.

"He's a member of the cabinet. There was no way the government could deny him that. He has a real political party and it gets real votes in the elections. He travels under a diplomatic passport and many of his aides have them as well. They carry their stuff through other countries and they never have to clear customs. They are under diplomatic protection.

"Now do you believe I know what's going on?" Amato was not angry about the situation. He understood that Beeker had to check out their information. It was a part of the job and he was simply cooperating.

"How do we find out some specifics about what he's up to now?"

"I have some people in the Cadozza camp."

"Spies?"

"Agents of the republic." Amato was testy about this one. "They know where we are. They'll come here as soon as they can. If we can wait for them . . ."

"No." Beeker had no intention of sitting for long in a camp

where he had already been attacked once. It was possibly a mistake that their first attackers hadn't succeeded. "We have to move on them. We have to start shaking them up."

"Do you think that your little force is going to accomplish what the guerrillas haven't been able to do in years? Just go in and get rid of Cadozza? Are you crazy?"

"No. Just confident."

Amato didn't argue with him.

"The man's spread out. He's got operations all over Central America, we know that from the testimony that Harry heard. His sources aren't in this region, they have to be in South America. His distribution is in the United States. It's just too much for us to cover."

Beeker was standing in the middle of the clearing, the rest of them sitting in a semicircle on the ground listening to him. "He's able to move around 'cause he thinks he's got a safe base, all of this province. It gives him an illusion of power, a sense of a home base that's impregnable. So we've got to show him the errors of his ways."

"I smell bombs," Marty said with a show of enthusiasm. "I taste bombs. I feel bombs!"

The little blond man's sudden rampage startled Amato, who looked with obvious wonder at the image of this skinny runt standing up with his arms held over his head, his face turned to the sky with a totally ecstatic expression.

"My new mortars? Huh, Beak, my new mortars could do them in, make them—"

"No."

As soon as Beeker said that, Appelbaum collapsed back onto the ground, deflated and depressed. "But the mortars would be perfect," he answered.

"They're not frightening enough."

"*My* mortars aren't frightening enough?" The very idea that his leader and friend Beeker would have such a low opinion of his abilities with a weapon left Marty in a state of shock. He took off his glasses and rubbed the pale skin on the bridge of his nose. This was obviously too much for the little man to stomach.

"When we want to wipe out Cadozza's camp, then we'll use your stuff," Beeker said to calm the guy's spirits. "Right now what we want is to scare him. You kill; Cowboy scares."

That got their attention. "The helicopter. There are a couple of those things in Nicaragua that are scaring the shit out of every anticommunist in the Western Hemisphere. It's supposedly only there and in Cuba. It's one of the reasons that the boys in Washington go crazy over the Sandinistas. It's too big a toy for their friends in Moscow to let little guys play with."

"And they know how to play with it."

"If Cadozza thinks that a Russian Hind-D is now in the hands of the guerrillas here in El Salvador, he's going to know he's in bigger trouble than he thought. He expected us to shoot at his choppers but not with one of our own. If the Sandinistas are crossing the borders in the kind of strength that would be coming with that thing, then he's got big problems. It'd be even worse if the commies had given the guerrillas their own. That would mean a major escalation of their involvement in this country and it would be something for the man to lose sleep over.

"So, we show him a Hind-D."

"An air strike," Cowboy said. He was just as enthusiastic as Marty about the idea of his own preferred equipment getting into the middle of things; he was just a little more subtle about it all.

"You got it." Beeker turned to Amato. "Let's look at the layout of the camp."

"This is it." He had spread out another one of his cloth maps on the hard dirt. His finger pointed to a town whose name was written in larger print than those of the other towns in its vicinity.

"Almost all of the villages of this area are abandoned. But this, Domingo, was the provincial capital. All of the original civilians have left. It's Cadozza's main base. All of his stuff is here—the arms, the treasury, all of it."

Amato brought another smaller map, which was on paper for a change. It had been sketched out in colored pen. "This is the layout of Domingo. It's a traditional scheme for this part of the world. The church and the governor's palace are on either side of the central square. They are the most important buildings in the city.

"On the other two sides are the old shops. There isn't a market in any real sense anymore. The only things that come in arrive in convoys from Cadozza's people on the coast, or by airplane and helicopter here." His finger moved to a blue-shaded area on the map. "This is the airport he uses."

"Hell, if there's a treasury in there, we don't want to take it out until we know just where," Cowboy said. "What about their ammunition dumps?"

"Same problem. They could be storing their stuff in the church, in the governor's palace, you name it. We don't know yet. We will, when my people can report in, but until then . . ."

"Until then the airport looks awfully appealing," Cowboy declared. "We don't need it, we have the bird, we could land it in the middle of the square if we need to later. But it would make life a little more dangerous and unappealing for Cadozza and his folks. I like it. Let's take it."

"So, why don't you?" That was all Beeker said. Amato folded up the map and stood to follow the Cherokee away from the group.

Cowboy was smirking, making some quick calculations in his head. Harry simply sat there, expressionless. Marty was sulking. "You have all the damn fun."

10

Cowboy had the one most valuable weapon in the world: surprise.

It was the one thing that there was never a defense against. You could have all the antiaircraft guns, all the artillery, all the manpower, in the world, but if you weren't ready when the time came, they were all as useful in a battle as a thin man's lifetime membership in Weight Watchers.

He flew the big Hind-D near ground level just to make sure that he maintained his advantage. If there happened to be anything as sophisticated as radar up here in the Salvadoran mountains, it wasn't going to discover the low-flying helicopter in time to take away Cowboy's big trump card.

The bird moved at near top speed. It was insanely reckless for anyone to fly a piece of equipment like this only inches over the treetops at this rate but to Cowboy it was just a little something to make sure he didn't get bored.

Cowboy fingered the controls for the big antitank missiles that were loaded onto the copter. Those were going to be his personal present to this asshole Cadozza. Cowboy was going to be glad to get a chance to use them. But he couldn't help thinking that—at least for him—this might not be the wisest thing in the world.

Cowboy had blind allegiance to Beeker. He truly did, and he reminded himself of it every day of the year. He knew that Beeker was his best friend in the world. They had saved one another's lives countless times over the years. Even before the team had gotten back together again, the two men had lived near each other, had gone fishing together, and Beeker had let Cowboy keep his planes on his property as a special favor.

As Cowboy kept telling himself, that was the most important thing in a man's life, that kind of loyalty to friends. Of course it was. But there were other things that were important in a man's life.

Like his coke.

Cowboy had this one big problem. He thought that what other people called reality was actually only a dream state, and a lethargic one at that. What Cowboy thought was reality was a great big buzz brought on by enough toots to burn a fire-eating path through his nostrils.

They'd all given up things to rejoin the team. Each and every one of them had something that he had to lose in order to mesh with the others. That's just the way it is. The problem for Cowboy was difficult, though. He thought his penance was bigger than any of the other guys'. He just had been forced to give up his coke.

Now here he was, flying an engine of destruction to make an attack on a man who was reputed to be one of the biggest dealers in the whole world.

Cowboy knew damn well that there was a shortage of his vital white powder back in the States. Prices had been skyrocketing, a sure sign that there was too much demand for the amount available.

But Cadozza was the man who could be bringing in enough of the nose candy to keep Cowboy happy for the rest of his natural life. And Cowboy was going to have to dry up this supply?

Cowboy hoped that Beeker didn't realize he still was taking his long walks at night, his nature tours during the day, and his afternoon meditations in order to sniff up enough coke to keep himself going. Cowboy respected the leader's absolute command in the field, but at home, hell, a man had to have some fun.

What if Cowboy was now facing the ultimate test? He was in the field, his leader had told him to bomb the headquarters of the best source of cocaine in the world, and he was going to suffer personally for it for the rest of his existence. What a dilemma! There is no easy way out for a fighter pilot.

Domingo came into sight quickly. The old Spanish colonial architecture didn't have many tall buildings here in such a provincial town. But the spire of the church and the upper story of the governor's palace made for definite identification of the place when they came into view over the jungle. In a few seconds there were a few more buildings he could see, and then the clearings for the farmland around the village were obvious as well.

He mentally recalled the map that Amato had had him study. The airstrip was going to be off to the northeast of the church steeple. That was his landmark.

The Hind-D was zeroing in fast. In a matter of seconds Cowboy saw the clearing. There was a modern asphalt runway. It seemed to contradict the ancient appearance of the town. He estimated it could handle all but the largest of aircraft. Cadozza had plans for this place. Too bad they were going to be sidetracked.

Cowboy flew over the strip once, at top speed. The roar of the engines sent the stunned men who were working in the area running. There were a couple of them silly enough to be shooting rifles up at the craft.

The Hind-D had enough armor on it to make those rifles about as effective as peashooters. Cowboy had spotted a number of small craft on the tarmac. Nothing terribly impressive, certainly nothing that was going to come up here and try to do him in. But he knew that eliminating them would be a fine little show for the boys on the ground. He'd start there.

Another target was just as obvious. There were some old American Sherman tanks. They weren't much use here in the jungle, and were probably only stored here for now. Maybe they were something that Cadozza thought he might use in his next chapter, a move on the coastal cities. Too bad, because Cowboy thought it might be important to get them out of the way.

The final target had impressed itself on his mind. It wouldn't take up one of the big AT-6 "Spiral" missiles. It could be handled with the four-barrelled 23-millimeter cannons that were attached to his pods.

Cowboy made his circuit—the whole lookover he'd accomplished had taken maybe 30 seconds—and headed back toward the airstrip. The last choice of target loomed up in front of his sites.

The petroleum supplies for the air base. There were three of them, large cylindrical structures. It must be a pain in the ass to keep them filled, since the fuel supply would have to be trucked into this remote locale.

Too bad.

Cowboy fired the cannons. Every fourth round was a tracer so a series of red streaks arced through the air directly at the target. Cowboy played the pip of the gunsite across the tanks. One after another they took the impact of the cannons' rounds and seemed to hesitate for a second, then they shuddered and then . . .

BOOOOOOM!!!!

The second tank exploded: BOOOOMMMMM!!!!

The third one must have contained more than the others. When it went off there was an explosion that sent a shock wave through the air so strong even Cowboy felt it as it rocked the helicopter.

BAAAAAMMMMMMMM . . .

The end of the airstrip was a mass of flames. The explosion of the third tank was so powerful that it actually sent up a mushroom cloud. Cowboy looked back and realized that he had cut that one awfully close. The cloud of smoke and flame had come too damn near his copter. Someday he'd make a bigger miscalculation than these few feet and it would be all over for him.

Someday.

This day he had better things to worry about, like those planes and tanks. The explosions had only added to his advantage over any possible defenders. They had seemed cataclysmic to the people near them. Everyone down there was probably running around paying attention to nothing else, and the cloud of smoke gave Cowboy a great shield.

His hands moved back to the controls for the AT-6 antitank missiles that the Soviets had so nicely produced for him. They called these babies Spirals. He could see why when he released them, sending each of the four toward a separate target with only a few seconds between their launchings.

The explosions weren't as big this time, nor as spectacular. But they were damned effective. First, a row of aircraft just blew away as though they were little-boy toys that some bully had come in and messed up. A single missile landed at the start of the line and there was a little burst of red flame and then, like dominoes, one after another of the planes caught on fire. A second Spiral started the whole process all over again farther down the line.

Then the tanks. One, then another, Spiral went on its deadly way toward the earth, and when it landed there were direct hits on two clusters of the Shermans. They flew apart, sending ragged pieces of metal through the air. No one could ever have believed that those were once the backbone of the American land forces. They were just toys that some bully didn't want you to play with anymore.

Cowboy sped away. His work wasn't just complete, it was perfect. He smiled to himself; that had been a damned good job, all right. A damn good job. It had taken him all of about three minutes to wipe out the general's game plan. He tried to think of how happy Beeker would be, how proud he should feel that he'd performed so well for the sake of the team's effort, and not even to glance on the idea that he might just have destroyed his own recreational budget by making his coke all the more expensive.

Even if he did know that he had done a perfect job, Cowboy wasn't about to brag about it. He landed the helicopter in the camp clearing and nonchalantly turned off the two big turboshaft engines. As they whined down, he calmly stepped out of the bird and easily walked over to where the others waited for him.

"Problem?" That's all Beeker asked when Cowboy got close enough to speak.

"Nope." That was Cowboy's only answer.

"Followed?"

"Nope."

"What did you get!" Marty was the one who just couldn't stand it any longer. "What! Tell me! I could have done it better. I could have gotten more, just a few little mortars and I could have gotten twice as much shit as you did."

The little blond man was stomping the ground with his feet, having a tantrum. "I should have been the one to do it. I'm the one who knows how to destroy things around here. *Really* destroy things. You just toss some things out of your window from up in the air. That doesn't count."

Harry came up and put a big hairy arm around Marty's shoulders, patting them gently a few times to calm the guy down. He looked at Cowboy and just rolled his eyes. There was just nothing to do with the runt when he got in one of these moods, and all they could ever hope to do was ignore him and let him get over it. Maybe.

"To answer the question, just for your information"—Cowboy was studying Beeker now—"even if you aren't the one who asked it, you might be interested in knowing that I took out a couple of tanks, set at least six aircraft on fire, and destroyed the entire fuel supply of the fucked-up place."

Beeker was ignoring Marty and now he seemed surprised that Cowboy evidently was going to throw his own temper tantrum. "I knew that," he said. "You already told me you did the job."

"Goddam Indians!" Cowboy swore in frustration. He was ready to go farther, but then realized that he was really just upset about his moral dilemma. There was nothing that Beeker would do about that, he'd never even be able to understand. In fact, it was worse. Beeker would have been happy that Cowboy had been forced to hurt the flow of drugs into the United States.

"Oh, forget it," he finally said. "Just forget it."

They had their midday meal: simple cheese sandwiches and some cold, leftover coffee. They'd all had so many other meals in the field that were so much worse that no one thought to complain.

"That attack will serve many purposes," Amato said while they were eating. "It will alert Cadozza that there are some very well armed guerrillas operating up here, too close to his base camp for his comfort. Your conservatives back in the United States will be horrified. They'll be worried that he's not doing the job if he can be so easily made vulnerable.

"There's a danger that they'll simply arrange for even more money for him, but I hope we'll have done our job so quickly that there won't be time for them to get the matériel here."

"Cadozza's equipment comes through legit channels," Beeker said, chewing his sandwich. "That means the Pentagon. That means it'll take a hell of a long time for anything to get here. He can probably replace the fuel himself, buy a few old planes on the black market, that sort of thing. But in terms of getting a shipment of the type of supplies he's getting from the United States, that'll take forever."

"Besides that," Amato continued, "it will get my people here to make their reports even faster. The raid will be so much news that they'll have to make contact. It's good. I want to talk to them before we go any farther."

"Your people can get in and out of Domingo that easily?" Harry asked. He seemed impressed.

"In the daytime my people have a great ability to move around." Amato was smiling; obviously he was pleased with himself. "I expect we'll hear from them very, very soon."

They were all willing to let Amato have his moment of assuredness. It'd help make up for the problem he'd had in the beginning. No one wanted this guy to fail, certainly not Beeker. They let his comments pass.

"You know, Beeker, the one thing that still gets to me is how the hell Delilah managed to get that thing here. I don't mean just to this part of the world. That I can see getting arranged. I mean, how'd she ever get it in the first place?" Cowboy was still questioning the powers of the strange woman in Washington.

"Supposedly, there are all kinds of rewards out there for one of these babies. You don't exactly walk into a showroom and say, 'Give me one of those.' "

Beeker got one of his stormy expressions on his face. He didn't like this conversation one bit. "I just suppose there's a damn good equivalent doing a job someplace down in Colombia about now. An American-made sweetheart with a communist at the controls."

"Are you trying to tell me we just went to the Russians and said, 'Let's swap?' Beeker, the world doesn't work that way."

"It does if you live in Washington."

The conversation was obviously finished.

The tropical night was heavy with humidity. Beeker stood looking out over the countryside, listening to the sounds of the nocturnal animals that had come out to look for food. There was a lot of killing in a jungle at night. Most of it was hidden during the day.

The big killers of the forest liked to work at night. The cats, the birds of prey, all rested during the daytime heat. But when the sun was gone, they came out, moving hungrily through the jungle, searching out the weaker members of the natural order.

It was the way the world worked.

Beeker knew that there was no way to pass judgment on it. That wasn't the point. That wasn't the point at all. It was just the way things were. The jaguar killed. The cat had no morals about it, he was hungry, his family needed food, he hunted, he found food, he brought it back. Life went on.

He could feel Amato approaching him from behind before he saw the Salvadoran. "Cigarette?" Amato asked.

"No, thanks," Beeker answered. He never had smoked.

The other man lit up. The sudden ember of his tobacco was a bright point in the darkness. Beeker couldn't help but register the possible danger. It was a perfect way for an enemy to track their camp. But if the guy was comfortable with it—and he knew that a trained Marine like Amato would be aware of what he was doing—then Beeker wasn't going to argue.

"Your friend the pilot is right. It's very strange for there to be such a helicopter here in El Salvador. There must be a story."

Beeker spat. "You know the kind of people who've gotten us all involved in this. You know we're not just dealing with getting rid of Cadozza because he's not a nice person. Hell, if the United States had wanted to just come in and off the asshole, we could have done it a long time ago. If they had really wanted to they would have arranged for a group of suckers like us to move right in here and do the job. There's more involved here."

Amato waited a minute before going on. "In Annapolis, when I went there, I was astonished by the way that some of the cadets acted. They liked their smoke, they had their little white powders.

"I always thought that they were spoiled brats. They didn't know that war wasn't a little field exercise they were going to play from headquarters, it was something real. The ones who thought like me, they were the ones that went into the Corps.

"We used to talk about the rest of them. They were dangerous, and the danger was directed at us. They were the ones that were going to be flying the big Navy jets that were supposed to give us air strikes, and they were going to be useless if they were too stoned to read a map."

"You got it. You got a tiny example of what's going on back there. The whole society is full of it—companies going to hell and back, stoned actors are the heroes of our children, coked-up singers are the ones the kids want to be like. It's all out of hand."

"So, even if it means that a couple of Russian—or Cuban or Nicaraguan—pilots might get their hands on the most advanced aircraft in your arsenal, this is a problem so large your government has no choice?"

"So they say," Beeker acknowledged. "So they say."

"Your man will give the Pentagon a full report on the Hind-D, then?"

"Hell, no." Beeker snorted. "The brass isn't smart enough to realize that an actual pilot might have something so important to say that they should pay attention. They probably had some high-tech dummies go over the bird with their instruments and their cameras. They're sure they already know more about it than Cowboy. You can't tell them differently."

There was another pause. But the topic had Amato going. "It really does bother you to have them flying one of your craft."

"Yeah," Beeker said. "It bothers me a lot."

"In a war like this, in a country such as ours, it's often necessary to have allies that aren't our first choice."

Beeker wasn't buying any of that. "Not for me it isn't. And I don't think it is for you either."

"There are two different things, my friend," Amato responded, without sounding like he was being defensive. "There are the times of survival when compromises are necessary and one takes any friend he can. Then there are the times when a force needs to consolidate. We aren't there—consolidating—in my country yet. We don't ask questions yet of people who would help us and we don't wonder how and why something useful came to get into our hands."

"Maybe for you—when you need to survive. I don't need to survive in this shit. I just need to do my job and go home." Beeker had answered quickly, but now there was something else on his mind. "Is that all you think about us, that we're just someone to help, and you think—"

"I think you and I are of like minds on many subjects, Beeker. I think we're friends. That's important right now. I just wanted to know about the helicopter. If it had been just for us, your people wouldn't have arranged it. But it was not that simple. I understand. What I'm saying to you is this: I don't care why it's here. I don't care why it's being used to get rid of Cadozza. I just want it and I want it to do that job."

He threw the cigarette to the ground and crushed it with his boot. "Besides. That machine is not the best weapon that's come here for us.

"You are."

11

If Rosie was going to *have* to compromise his morals, this was as good a way as any other he'd ever heard of.

He was sitting in the living room of Jezebel Strauss's apartment over the Boston Club. Outside, El Paso was alive with the street life of any big American city. But the sounds of children playing when they should have been home doing their homework, or the shouts of drunken couples arguing, the squeals of car wheels taking corners too fast, were all far away.

Here there was just the beauty of Jezebel. And that was some beauty, Rosie thought to himself. The woman was walking through the apartment naked.

Women should be like this, he thought to himself. They should be naked, they should be ready, they should be willing. He sipped on the Scotch he'd been drinking and lingered on that profound thought.

Rosie knew he was giving just the impression he wanted to. He was a good, loving man who was in the criminal life. He was hard, capable of taking on any two-bit punk like that Stick and doing him in if it was necessary. But he was in this for the good life.

He had painted a picture of himself that Jezebel was accepting without any hesitation. He had climbed up the ladder of crime with his ability to use his fists and a gun. He'd set up a drug empire in the black ghettoes of Buffalo and other upper New York State cities. His was an empire that wasn't big enough to give the really important crime syndicates any problems. It made sense that he could exist without knowing any of them. He wouldn't have been giving them any problems.

Black businessmen of just about any sort were willing to take the backseat. They thought they had made it when they had a bit of money, more than they knew how to spend in a year. Didn't make any difference if it was an honest business or drugs. The blacks were used to second best.

There were exceptions, of course. There were some places like Harlem where the black gangsters were so powerful that they could have blown away some of the little Eye-talian fools down in Little Italy. Rosie wondered if that might not be a life for him. He could see himself on the streets of his hometown of Newark, New Jersey. Big bad Roosevelt Boone walking around wearing these silly clothes all the time, being driven in a huge stretch Cadillac limousine with a couple of fine foxy ladies on either side of him, feeling him up constantly in hopes he might throw them an extra hundred-dollar bill.

Nah, it didn't work. There was something inside Rosie that kept that kind of daydream from ever being real. Any other black kid he'd grown up with would have taken that way out if he'd had Rosie's intelligence and his physical strength. It was the most success that any of them had ever even dreamed of back then.

None of them had wanted to be doctors, lawyers, politicians, not even sports heroes. They'd wanted to be pimps, they wanted to run the biggest numbers game in Newark, they wanted to learn how to be hit men. They were all probably dead now.

That saddened Rosie and made him take another drink of his

Johnnie Walker Black Label. It was true, but it was still sad to think of all those dead young men, their bodies littering the alleyways of a dying city like Newark.

Rosie could have gone that route, no doubt about it. But instead he found himself sitting in El Paso, Texas, with Jezebel walking around nude. Something had stopped him. Something had altered his course, his direction.

The war. Of course there had been the war. And there had been Beeker. Things happened to men in war. Only sometimes were there people nearby who made any sense of them. Beeker had done that for Rosie. So had the rest of the team that had come to be known as the Black Berets. They had made sense out of chaos. They had given him an identity that made more sense than Black/Cherokee/Jew/White. And without them he had slipped back into the chasm of absurdity.

Rosie finished off his drink and sighed. Like all the others, he'd tried to make it on his own, submerge himself in something different. But, like the others, he'd discovered that it simply and purely couldn't work. There was only himself and the Black Berets. There was only life on the farm and life in the field. This was the only way any of them had to make sense of it.

So, Rosie's acting as the big drug pusher from Buffalo was only an assignment. It wasn't something that was ever going to be real. If that was so, he'd better get his act back together.

"Girl, bring that cute little body of yours back over here for me," he called out to Jezebel.

She turned, forgetting her task, and stared at him. There was that wistful expression on her face, one that was mixed with fear and joy, disbelief and adoration. It said one thing: "Not again." But it didn't say it so loudly that she didn't move across the thick carpet and stand in front of Rosie.

He moved his hands up to her waist, feeling the tautness of her muscles, and pulled her gently toward him.

"Mm-mum!" he said playfully. "Finest little ass from here to Hollywood."

"Don't talk dirty to me," she said, pulling away, but clearly not meaning it, obviously loving it.

He slapped her large and firm rear. "We gonna go to that meeting now?" He knew it was time for it, but he didn't want to press it too hard. He didn't want to lose his advantage.

"You want to do that?" Her voice was slightly disappointed. "Yes, actually"—she looked over to the clock and agreed—"we should go."

Rosie felt as though he had pushed a magic button in the middle of Jezebel's mind. It was like she was some kind of chameleon. The sexy little lady he'd been planking these past couple of days was gone. Suddenly he saw the hard, calculating woman who had been running the Boston Club the first day he'd entered the doorway.

She moved quickly now, no longer distracted by his presence. It was probably the way a business executive acted when his little time out with a call girl was done. All fun and games while he was paying the meter, but then that same psychology that had allowed him to earn the money to afford the extravagant entertainment would have come over him and he would have reverted back to his real life.

Jezebel wasn't at all coy while she dressed. Nor was she dressing for Rosie the way she had been before, asking him what colors he liked, if he enjoyed the touch of silk or preferred the feel of cashmere.

He watched her, impressed, and remembered all those books they sold nowadays for females. *Dress for Success, Power Lunching,* crap like that. It certainly appeared as though she'd read them.

When she was done with her efficient preparations, Jezebel looked over at him. "You better do something with yourself too. Your best suit. Uncle Herman likes suits on people he does business with."

That was the kicker, the real kicker. Here Rosie had walked into the Boston Club and thought it was just a place to begin the contacts, but he had actually discovered the center of it all.

96

All of it. When Jezebel talked about "Uncle Herman," she wasn't joking around, she wasn't making believe, talking about some john or some nice old man. It was her *uncle*. Uncle Herman Strauss. He had only recently gotten it through his thick head that this black honey could have a Kraut relative.

Rosie had heard of white men visiting the woodpile before, of course he had. But this was a little role reversal going on here. It was momma did the nasty visit. She must have been over in Germany right at the end of the Second World War. She found herself a starving German man and she brought him back home. A little early women's lib, Rosie decided.

Rosie went back over Jezebel's conversations. Yes, yes, it had all been there. That thing about putting together her momma's connections and her daddy's and getting a real big plus from it all. Momma might have been a nurse in the service, but she was a black woman who knew her way around the streets. Daddy would have been a man who had learned the hard ways to get by during the war. Momma had the contacts in the ghetto that could eventually have led to the highest levels of syndicated crime. Daddy had the scars that let a man know how to survive. He'd also had all the good German training in business and organization. Oh, they must have been a great team.

Give them a little border between Mexico and the U.S. to play with, a hefty and growing market for some drugs, a few connections, and they were in business. It had been big enough to set up the generations that had followed.

They went down the stairs when Rosie was as well dressed as Jezebel insisted he had to be. There was a car waiting for them, a white Lincoln. Another black man that Rosie had met before when he'd used Jez's car for his own transportation was standing there. He'd told Rosie his name was Clarence. Now, he opened the door and held it for them without speaking a word. Rosie imagined he'd seen a lot of guys coming and going just like Rosie.

Rosie had also noticed from the very beginning that Clarence was packing. At least a revolver in a shoulder holster, and there were probably a couple other little goodies around besides. A knife in his boot; a derringer in another holster in the back of his belt? Clarence wasn't a man who had been hired to take many chances.

Jezebel hadn't been very forthcoming about herself. The time she'd spent with Rosie had been easygoing and very, very sexual. The girl knew what she wanted. So long as Rosie was giving it to her good—and of course he was—then he was welcome. If he was going to give it as good as he had been for as many times as he'd been willing, then she evidently felt he was owed a favor. That was it.

They drove through El Paso and crossed the Rio Grande into Mexico, only slightly inconvenienced by the formality of going through a little customs check. It was obvious that both the American and Mexican border officials knew Jezebel and Clarence as well.

Then they were in Ciudad Juárez. Rosie had studied the other, darker side of El Paso from his hotel window. But the reality of the poverty would have been overwhelming to anyone who hadn't grown up in a neighborhood like his own. The children in the streets had none of the fresh-washed look that the American kids had. They had distended bellies from hunger, their clothing seemed to be mainly made up of discarded and utterly out-of-place celebrity T-shirts. What was a kid in Juárez doing wearing Bruce Springsteen's face on his chest?

But as soon as the kids had passed that age, they had a different look about them. Rosie could see it as he watched them out of the Lincoln's windows. There were kids as young as twelve who had gone through a transformation. They were one of two kinds—and the separation didn't pay any attention to gender. There were those boys and girls who were hard. They'd either be the criminals or else the ones who'd take out their anger at the world on their own unwelcome children someplace down the line. Then there were the ones who'd seen the one way out of this, if only for a minute. They were the ones who were selling it.

There were prostitutes on nearly every single corner of Juárez. There were old ladies, there were beautiful women, there were soulful-looking boys. They were perfectly clear about the only way they knew to escape what role the world was trying to impose on them. They had figured out that their bodies were the only commodity that could possibly have value in this life and they were ready to trade them.

Someplace, Rosie was sure, there must be middle-class neighborhoods in Juárez. But he'd be damned if he had ever been able to find them. There was sure to be someplace where the insurance agents, the middle-level government bureaucrats, the car salesmen, lived in something that wasn't either squalor or ostentatious wealth. But he'd never seen it.

The Lincoln pulled up in front of a modern home on the edge of the city, but not too far out. The buildings on this street weren't big spreads, they were close together, separated by high walls that underlined the wealth of the inhabitants.

Clarence opened their door again, never having spoken a word the entire time they were in the car. Rosie thought that was fine, he'd just play along. Jezebel seemed a little anxious, as though not quite confident that she'd completed her transformation. She threw him a glance, looking like she wasn't sure, either, if this big black man didn't have too much power over her, so much power that he might make it impossible for her to do her job.

Rosie sensed her anxiety. "Strut your stuff, baby, show me what you're really made of."

It did the trick. She smiled, seemed to relax, and walked toward the huge front door.

The house was done up in a more tasteful style than Rosie had ever dreamed of seeing in Juárez. He knew little about such things, but he assumed that much of the furniture was honestly antique. There was a feel to a lot of the pieces that made it seem a pretty sure thing. The tiles on the floor were hand painted, he was positive of that. The walls were the old adobe of the colonial era, lovingly and perfectly whitewashed.

The entry, where they had been greeted by a heavy but surprisingly spry old Mexican woman, was spacious. Everything in this hacienda was that way, Rosie realized. He suddenly understood that this house must have been the oldest in the region. It was the main house of what had been an enormous spread back in the old days. The other structures on the block were intruders, allowed entry by some previous owner who most certainly did not have the same taste and appreciation as the current resident.

They went through the entry and walked directly into a beautiful open plaza. There was a riot of plants here, many of them blooming with exotic colors. In a nod to modern times the plaza had been roofed with glass. It not only allowed the air to be cooled, but it also served as a cage for the flock of parrots that cawed from the limbs of some of the tree-sized growth.

They walked past a large fountain that dominated the center of the plaza and now entered still another room. The air-conditioning was stronger, cooler, here. It was a traditional living room. Large sofas done in a mission-era style formed a sitting area. The maid gestured for them to sit here.

"A drink?" she offered.

"No, thank you. Perhaps coffee," Jezebel suggested.

"Of course."

"And Uncle Herman knows I'm here?"

"Yes, of course, Señorita Strauss."

The household was run with a military efficiency that would have impressed even Beeker. Rosie sat silently while he watched the woman pour two cups of thick Mexican coffee into small cups of porcelain that sat on matching saucers. As soon as she had delivered them to the two guests, she moved to a corner of the room and pushed a small button on the wall that was so well concealed he hadn't yet noticed it. But he did notice that there was a pistol under the waistband of the maid's skirt.

He sipped the coffee and waited to see how this scene would finish. The timing was perfect. As soon as he and Jezebel had leisurely finished their refreshments, a tall blond man of about fifty-five strode into the room. "My dear Jezebel," he exclaimed grandly, "it is always a pleasure to see you."

Jez stood up and accepted a paternal hug from the man. Rosie took in the sharply perfect creases on his slacks, the curl of his shirt collar, and the thick but balanced knot of his tie and realized that this was a man who would have a hard time with anything that wasn't done exactly right. He must have a hell of a time dealing with the kind of people he was forced to deal with. But his profits were certain to be so large, so enormous in fact, that Rosie wasn't going to lose any sleep worrying about him.

"Uncle Herman Strauss, let me introduce Mr. Roosevelt Boone."

"How are you, Mr. Strauss?" Rosie was tempted to play up his street-nigger act, but didn't think it was necessary despite the fun he could have doing it.

"My sweet Jezebel tells me that you are a fine businessman from Buffalo, Mr. Boone," Strauss remarked taking Rosie's handshake. "She thinks that you and I might have business to do. I'm afraid I haven't had the pleasure of knowing you before. But then the times have been difficult for many people in this area of endeavor. We've had a number of new and previously unheard-of customers coming to us."

Rosie could tell that Strauss wasn't exactly upset by the prospect. "Well, a man's got a market, makes a good living at it, and then discovers that he can't find the goods to meet his demand. Then a man hears that there are folks down in this part of the world who can help him out. Not a lot he can do but check into it. It's just a nice coincidence that I met up with Jezebel so quickly, saved a lot of time."

"Yes, yes," Strauss said, a plastic smile on his face. "My dear niece has been helpful here."

Rosie wondered if Uncle Herman knew just how helpful Jezebel could be. "Well, why don't we talk some real business?" He had finally decided to stay on the track with this dude.

"Of course." Uncle Herman wasn't at all upset about keeping

101

the conversation on a financial footing. "We have a menu of goods, actually, Mr. Boone. Let me show them to you."

Herman snapped his fingers. Out of nowhere a young man appeared. He had the coffee-colored skin of a Mexican. Even Roosevelt Boone, fresh from days of keeping a woman like Jezebel happy, knew that this guy was beautiful. He suddenly remembered paintings that had been reproduced in Tsali's textbooks on classical art. This guy deserved to be in one of them. He had perfect posture, he moved with a flowing kind of grace. His body was well muscled without any of the bulk that Rosie had himself.

Rosie took in the young man's appearance and then looked back to Uncle Herman. He knew something about the Kraut now. There was only one reason why a servant as handsome as this was around. Uncle Herman liked his boys.

The young man handed Rosie a folder. It surprised him at first, he couldn't figure it out. It felt like an actual menu from some extra-fancy restaurant. Rosie opened it up and couldn't help but whistle at the way these guys carried through with their class act.

The goddam thing *was* a menu. In perfect handwriting were columns listing the substances for sale, minimum and maximum quantities and prices.

Rosie looked up at Uncle Herman. "I have never seen anything like this." His laugh showed his acknowledgement of the fancy touch.

Uncle Herman nodded his acceptance of the compliment. "Please, make sure you notice the notation on the bottom of the page."

Rosie went back to the menu and saw what Strauss was talking about. In the same flowing penmanship someone had written:

All Payment in Gold Bullion

Uncle Herman didn't like to take chances. "You mean to tell me that you don't take good old-fashioned American currency?" Rosie said.

"Never." Strauss wasn't leaving any room for misunderstanding here. "We deal on the international markets. There have been problems when American customers have indulged in their other hobbies—counterfeiting, for instance. But that isn't really the main concern. My suppliers need gold. There is no option."

"I've never dealt in gold before," Rosie said.

"There is no real problem," Strauss assured him. "There is no longer a restriction on the purchase of gold in this country. You'll find yourself able to buy the quantities necessary at many different traders. I suggest you go to Houston, perhaps Dallas, for your transaction. If you doubt my references, which I would understand if you felt it necessary, then go to New York City. After all, we aren't going to be doing our trades this afternoon."

"No, no, of course not." Rosie said. He already knew that the gold would be easy enough to get. But he'd be doing his banking in Shreveport. Strauss didn't have to know that there was enough of the stuff in the Berets' safe to cover more than adequately the expense of the transactions.

Rosie gave Strauss a quick look and realized this was probably the younger brother, the quick one, probably dragged out of war-torn Germany by Jezebel's daddy, taught the ropes, set up, and in place to take over when it was finished with.

Complete with another black woman just like her momma, who was sitting at the door of the Boston Club and who had a way to hear what was happening on the streets, make those connections that would have been impossible for anyone else to make.

Too bad, Rosie realized, that he hadn't figured out that his valuable niece's taste for Rosie was blinding—blinding enough that it allowed her to overlook things and let in a man like him. He couldn't really get it together to feel sorry for this dude, but it was obvious to him that his was a deadly blindness.

"We have the materials that you need, Mr. Boone. We have them in great quantities, in fact. There is an unfortunate situation in the world markets, however. At least it's unfortunate for you. The goods have greatly inflated in price recently. We have no alternative but to pass that inflation on to our customers."

"Just tell me what we're talking here. I got hungry people up north in Buffalo. Hungry."

Strauss smiled.

"But I got to tell you," Rosie added, leaning back in his seat, "I have some very real worries about all this. See, my sources tell me that what shit does get into this country is all coming up through some people in El Salvador."

Strauss wasn't going to bite. "I don't question all of the activities of my suppliers. They are more than a little trustworthy. They've proven themselves to me."

"But not to me," Rosie insisted. "If you got this through a connection down there, I don't know if your promises are going to be any good."

"What do you mean by that?" Strauss was actually angry at the idea that his ability to produce the materials at issue could be questioned.

Rosie reached into his coat jacket and pulled out a clipping. "Seems there's been lots of trouble down there. Now, on the streets where I live, we don't know a whole lot about international politics and could care less. But I hear things, I remember things. If this is where you're going to get my shit, I think you're going to have trouble."

Herman Strauss picked up the piece of newsprint and studied it for a moment. A whole list of emotions came over his face. There was disbelief, anger, and a little fear, one after the other.

"My sources will not fail either of us, Mr. Boone. I promise you that."

He threw the paper down on the desk where they could all read its headline:

104

CADOZZA BASE BOMBED

ADVANCED RUSSIAN AIRCRAFT IN COMMUNIST STRIKE

OFFICIALS FEAR FOR LEADER'S POSITION
IN SALVADORAN CIVIL WAR

12

Harry never minded being on guard duty. Never. It was second nature to him. The usual hours during which usual people slept were meaningless to Harry. Being alone was the normal state for him.

He didn't mind the jungle either. He was used to it. It might have been well over ten years ago that he last stood in the rain forests of Southeast Asia, but they had become a second home to him. Here, in the Salvadoran mountains, he felt fine.

His eyes were adjusted to the vague moonlight. His ears took in the night sounds of life and death. He was like a human computer, not worried, not overly tense, just accepting the input he was receiving, recognizing it was the way things should be. He sat as far from where the others slept as he could, so the sounds of their breathing wouldn't interfere with his reception of other noises that could be much more serious than a few snores.

It was well after midnight. He didn't expect much. But then you never did. He thought about that, about all the nice stories

106

and books written about carefully orchestrated battles of logical numbers of men wearing identifiable uniforms as they marched over clearly defined terrains. That was what seemed impossible to Harry.

He sat there and wondered about other things that were strange to him. The vague memory of that story he'd heard about the blond woman was foremost in his mind. She had become an obsession with him, he knew it.

He also knew that the ideas that floated in his mind were impossible. The first instinct that had hit him was that he'd like to kill her. He'd like to strangle her. He'd like to shove a knife deep into her throat, or shoot a bullet into the side of her head. That same instinct was the one that told him that all people in war broke their most sacred vows at one time or another, but it didn't mean they should all be forgiven.

But another wave of emotion and desire had come over him, and it was stronger. He wanted to make love to her; he wanted to hold her and have her love him back. He couldn't figure it all out, but there was some kind of mutual forgiveness he thought they might be able to offer each other. If they could be together . . .

But the thoughts couldn't move much beyond that point.

There was a sound that was so minor few other men would have heard it. But Harry did. It might have been a big cat stepping on a branch and breaking it. Harry knew it was much more likely that it was a human being trying to be quiet as he moved through the bush.

He took the Russian rifle in his hand and fondled it. All ideas of sex with a beautiful woman were gone now. Now there was just him and this beautiful piece of machinery. They were just waiting for the arrival of the intruder. They were going to be making wonderful sounds together if Harry was right.

He didn't need to tense his muscles to ready himself. Harry was too good a warrior for that. The very fact that he sent out the silent messages to his body was enough. He could even let his eyes blink occasionally. He didn't have to worry about losing anything with a split-second mistake. Harry was trained. He was ready. The other guy better be too.

There was another sound, closer. It wasn't wood breaking this time, it was a suction noise, as though some heavy animal —a man, a jaguar—had misstepped into some mud. There was plenty of mud in the region. Not many jaguars.

Harry lifted the AK-47 up to his shoulder and put his eye to the Starlite scope that was attached to the barrel. His sight was suddenly changed.

The world became a weirdly hazy purple through the lens. There were shapes that were now much more distinct than they had been to his naked eye. He could make out the branches of bushes and trees, the shape of the rocks that stuck up in between them at certain points. There was nothing he couldn't discern with the wonders of the modern technology he had with him now.

Then he heard a voice. *"Agua."*

Harry let the rifle droop. That was the code that Amato had given them. It was only going to be used by his agents from Cadozza's compound when they came to make their report. It was specifically chosen to be ambiguous. They could just claim to be looking for drinking water if there was any chance meeting with another group beside Amato's.

Harry didn't put the AK-47 away, though. He'd had too much previous experience with people who found out little things like passwords. He waited. Then a body came through the bush.

He didn't want to believe it.

He brought the rifle back up to his shoulder and looked through the infrared. The world went purple again. It made everything seem surreal. He didn't need color to do that. What he saw was doing that already.

It was her.

The blond woman.

She was standing on the edge of the compound. His hands

108

got sweaty all of a sudden. There was a nervous tic in the muscles of his trigger finger. He had to will it not to pull backward.

He stood. He walked toward her. There wasn't a fire left. They'd put it out before the others went to bed. Even burning the driest hardwood meant some smoke but the canopy dispersed that. But at night the embers of an open fire would be a beacon luring on the enemy.

He had a flashlight attached to his belt. He took it off its hook and his thumb pushed the control forward. The light shone directly in her face, blinding her after the darkness she'd grown used to.

"Agua," she repeated, lifting an arm up to shield her tender eyes from the assaulting beam. *"Agua."*

Harry stood there. His rifle was in his other hand. He studied her, the gold hair that cascaded down and the supple body that was apparent even under the loose-fitting khaki clothes she was wearing.

"Yeah," he said. *"Agua."* He went to wake up the sleeping men.

Angela de la Croix was introduced to the others. "I'll be missed," she'd said. "I have to get back soon."

They'd quickly gotten some coffee going over a chunk of burning C-4 explosive. They shielded the flare of light with their bodies. The water had boiled quickly and they were sitting in a small circle with the woman. All of them but Harry. Harry was back on guard duty.

When they were all seated and ready, Angela began her report, talking directly to Amato.

"You've made him very upset. He doesn't know if he's more angry that you did get his planes and tanks or that you might have gotten his money. The one thing he does know is that he's grateful that you didn't get him."

"What damage did the attack do?" Cowboy asked. He wanted his moment of glory and got it as she fed back an inven-

109

tory of destruction that was precisely the same as his own report.

"And the blame? Who's he blaming?" Amato was anxious to have that question answered.

"The Chequipac Liberation Front." Angela smiled. "He had to come up with something and he had to do it fast. The American reporters went crazy. There were a group of them there, especially from the right-wing press. They were terrified of the attack—they're the kind that love the idea of a revolution, but hate the reality of it. They demanded to know how their beloved general could be so hurt by the guerrillas that they'd convinced themselves were already defeated.

"The Chequipac fit the bill perfectly. They are new, fresh, more mysterious, and therefore more upsetting to the types of people who worry about the unknown.

"The Russian helicopter was his best way out. He went on a rampage about it. It was proof, he said, that the Cubans were involved now. Only they would know how to operate such a weapon. He used it as an excuse to demand American intervention."

"So, our cover is now even better known and the whole world knows about us." Amato was pleased and made it obvious.

"That much is accomplished," Beeker admitted. "But now we've got to move to the next step. Using this fake leftist group to get him good and final. What's his schedule? When can the *terrorists* make their next move?"

Angela answered the question, even though Beeker had asked it of Amato. "You have to do something more. You have to legitimize the Front totally. You also have to remove his entire apparatus. If you just eliminate Cadozza, there's too much in place for another man to come in and run."

Beeker stared at her. It was obvious he didn't like this new element entering into the decision making. He was already pissed enough that Delilah and some unseen, unknown figures in Washington were pulling as many strings as they were. He wanted it clean, clear-cut. It was the way he always wanted things.

Working with Amata was . . . okay. He was a jarhead. He understood a battle, a plan, a means of action. Working with the Berets was always fine, especially since they were under his command. He didn't want another skirt in the action, though, especially not one who was so damned insistent on coming up with the ideas.

Amato didn't seem to sense Beeker's reactions. "All right, then, we'll plan. What do you suggest?"

"Screw this," Beeker snarled. "What the hell is this 'Let's plan' shit? We don't need a goddam consciousness-raising group to figure out when and how and what we attack."

Amato hesitated. He ran a finger through the earth in front of him, right along the surface; it was just a motion to get time. He knew what the problem was now and he was trying to figure out a way to solve it without getting anyone's dander up. "Look, Beak, Angela's another agent. Equal in rank to me. I know you see things differently. You think I'm the commander in the field. But it's not so. If anything, it's the other way around."

Beeker studied Amato for a moment and saw that he'd painted the guy into a corner. He was sorry to have done that and begrudgingly looked over to Angela, clearly waiting for her to go on now that her position was better defined. He wasn't going to rub it into Amato; she wasn't going to rub in into Beeker. Her voice was businesslike.

"Our task is not just to eliminate Cadozza, but to make sure that his operation goes with him. The issue isn't just this supposed military man who's turned himself into a mobster, it's that an entire segment of our military is now a criminal operation, manipulating our diplomatic corps, our government, anything it wants to. There are plenty of fools underneath Cadozza who'd take his place in a second. We have to make sure there's nothing worth taking."

"Another helicopter attack?" Cowboy said hopefully.

"No, not now. They've already brought in more sophisticated antiaircraft defenses. There are heat-seeking missiles that might prove too dangerous. I couldn't discover just what kinds there were, but if they're the best, your helicopter might have problems now."

"Bombs," Marty said, wistfully, so quietly that the rest of them almost didn't hear him. "Bombs could take them all out, and their missiles right along with them."

"That, or the mortars I see you have. That would do. But carefully timed. We have to make sure that Cadozza is there. And there's something else, another piece to the puzzle. I've gotten to meet most of Cadozza's compatriots. They're the usual ones, the ones from the gangs in the United States, the growers from Colombia and Ecuador. But there's one who seems to be more important than the rest. He's due in in a couple days on a sudden and unexpected trip. He has Cadozza just as worried as your attack. I don't understand why or how. But there's something there we have to wait for and identify."

"Wait!" Beeker spat out his most hated word.

"There's no option now," Angela repeated. "It has to be done. This is like a bad weed. You can't just take off the top, you have to get the root. Cadozza's the poisonous blossom— you have no idea how deadly a man he is—but the rest of it is just as important. Surely they told you that."

"They told me lots of shit," Beeker said, standing.

Angela was thinking again. "It would be sad to waste all this available manpower," she agreed. "I think the Chequipac Liberation Front could be even more valuable if it made still another attack, but at a different target. You should arrange to leave more obvious evidence of your presence, the kind of things that the American and European media can use to prove you exist.

"It's of the greatest importance to everyone concerned that when Cadozza is . . . eliminated, it must be done by some group that's known, and in a way that the real guerrillas can't

112

claim credit for it. If we let them do that, it will be another coup in their campaign."

"And you suggest what?" Beeker demanded.

"Emanuele, why not attack the roads leading up to the camp? True, most of Cadozza's drug trade is by air. But we could isolate this camp of his even better with a few well-planned assaults. We do want to have the entire thing clean, we don't want to leave it in place for the leftists as a base any more than we want any one of Cadozza's aides to be able to take over the financial realities."

"True," Amato said. "It's something to keep these fine men . . . occupied for the next few days."

"When this is all done, I have a file of things about him that will make many people very interested. He will be utterly discredited when I'm done. This is one operation that will be totally successful, believe me."

That was the end of the planning. Amato and Beeker agreed they'd work out the details in the morning. Marty could hardly contain himself. He just *knew* this was going to mean bombs. Harry looked at him and sighed. The guy was like a little kid who'd just heard that he'd won a year's pass to see all the Walt Disney movies he'd ever wanted.

There was a bustle as people moved around, no longer needing to be seated formally for the meeting. Marty got up and walked to the mortars that still were lined up in the middle of the compound. He took out a rag and wiped them, one after the other, just as willing to polish his own toys as Cowboy would have been to clean up his new helicopter.

Beeker was still all business. He would be. Cowboy was the one who changed the most. That was normal. There was a Latin lady in the camp and it wouldn't make a damn bit of difference to him that she was blond. Not in the least.

Harry took up his rifle and went back to the perimeter of the compound. He looked back out over the night and thought about the flier and his compulsion.

Cowboy had to have Latin ladies. Cowboy just loved Latin

ladies the way he couldn't ever learn to love any other kind of woman. He sure made that obvious enough, and not just with the way he looked in their eyes or studied their bodies. The stupid guy married them. One after another, Cowboy had taken a procession of Latin women to the altar.

When he was under the influence of Latin charms, Cowboy wasn't sensible. You couldn't ever talk straight to him. It wasn't an easy thing, like a schoolboy infatuation. It was something that took over his entire being.

The biggest problem with it all was one small flaw in Cowboy's version of loving: He might have liked *getting* married; he never had any intention of *staying* married. It was the romance, the courtship, and the high ceremony of the actual event that got to him. Of course, he liked the honeymoon a lot as well. But after that? Forget it.

Cowboy had walked out on women as far north as Minnesota and as far south as Tierra del Fuego. There were more Mrs. Cowboys standing around pissed off about being jilted than just about any other kind of woman in the world.

Beeker had finally imposed one rule that Cowboy had followed, not happily either. He demanded that Cowboy never marry any more women in Louisiana or the neighboring states of Texas, Oklahoma, or Arkansas. They were too close to home, that was all there was to it. There were too many daddies out there, who would be too pissed off that their baby girls had been left sleeping in their marriage beds, to risk it.

But this was Central America. Cowboy was on a free rein. There was a Latin-born lady and she was his for the taking, Harry figured. Just as well.

"You don't like the plans?"

Harry froze a little when he heard the voice talking to him so close by. His attention had all been focused in the other direction. He was disappointed in himself that he had let her move up on him this way.

"Doesn't make any difference to me." That's all he wanted to say to this woman.

They stood silently for a moment. Then she went on: "You said nothing at all during the meeting."

"Meeting? Hell, that was all between you and Beeker. I don't have anything to do with that stuff. I just follow his orders."

"Blindly?"

"I never did find a better way to do it."

"I'm surprised. Usually a big man like yourself is the kind who wants to be independent, wants to put in his thoughts, demands to be heard."

"I'm not that type. I'm fine, just listening to what Beeker has to say."

"Your pilot friend seems to want to have a great deal to say about many things."

He couldn't help smile at that. So Cowboy had already made the moves on her. "Don't you like him?"

"He's not my type." She moved closer.

He could sense her body and the image of her curves and her softness came back to him even though he wasn't looking at her. "He's a nice guy." That was all he could get out.

"Blond on blond isn't very exciting to me, that's all. I'm hardly a prude. But I want more. A bigger man. A darker man. A man more powerful than myself."

Harry's cool was gone now. He knew the woman was putting the moves on him. He wasn't like Cowboy, he didn't know how to respond instantly. He wasn't at all sure he wanted to.

"I heard about you and that Cadozza." He said it as much for himself as for her. *I know about you* was his message.

She didn't seem to receive it. "He's a pig. A despicable pig. But you heard about me, huh? I'm certainly a lot different than I used to be. Yes, the war has changed me." There was a quietness in her voice. It was the voice of a young woman remembering a nearly forgotten time. Harry thought about that. He remembered different times himself.

"My turn, Harry." It was Cowboy. He wasn't talking in a friendly style, that was obvious. And it was not his turn for guard duty. Harry was up for it till dawn. But the Greek knew what was going on. Cowboy, realizing he'd struck out, saw that Harry had a chance to get a piece of ass and he was all set to do everything he could for a buddy, even if it meant helping him get into a skirt that just shut down on Cowboy himself.

Harry felt like arguing—a little bit. More of him wondered about this blond woman. He nodded to Cowboy and walked back toward the center of the camp. By now the rest of them had moved back to their sleeping bags. Harry had ignored Angela. He sat on the ground and really couldn't have known if she'd been following him. He couldn't have known—but he did.

She was beside him in a matter of seconds.

"How did you get this assignment?" he finally asked.

She waited a moment before answering; she knew perfectly well what he was really asking. *How did a nice girl like you . . .* "I was very young when it started. Only fifteen or so. My parents were middle class. They were the kinds of people for whom the revolution meant little. They'd gain little; they only had a little to lose. They watched the politics of El Salvador from a kind of distance, not believing that such things as parties and guerrillas and right-wing hit squads could get them.

"Of course, they were wrong. They were very wrong.

"There were some people of Cadozza's party who wanted my father to join. We lived in a village not too far from the capital. They came often and talked to him; finally they began to threaten him. He refused to believe that an honest political party could resort to such tactics. He told them to go away.

"They did. But their friends came back in a few days and they murdered my father in the middle of the village square. We were never able to prove who it was, but we knew, of course we knew."

Harry hated times like this. He knew he should do something, put an arm around Angela's shoulder the way he might do to Marty to calm him down, but Harry felt funny about women, especially women in need. He just sat silently.

She either took it as an expression of interest, or else had her own reasons for wanting to go on and get this out.

116

"My two brothers, a little older than I, were incensed. They would join the leftists. If the right wing could do that—could terrorize a man like our father—then their enemies had to be the good people. So they went into the mountains. I've never heard from them again.

"I knew that life was more complicated than that. I soon saw that I had been right. Guerrillas had to make an attack on a target close to the capital. Our village was perfect. Only a month or two after the right-wing squads came and performed their murder, the guerrillas came. They were no better.

"I hid. My mother didn't have time. They raped her—many times. They raped her and then they killed her. After these events I knew that the only hope was to find a way to control all the forces in our country that were so out of control. There had to be a way to respect human life, to honor human dignity.

"But I also knew that I had none left. I had hidden while my mother was raped. I was hardly a blameless person. I moved to the capital and I found a room. I began to work in the government, I lied about my age and got a job in the offices of the central police. There came a time when they needed a very special volunteer.

"El Salvador is at war. Morals are a luxury we can't afford. I had no family left to dishonor. I offered.

"It seems there was a man, a businessman who used a façade of respectable trading to import great numbers of weapons. He didn't care to whom they were sold. Left wing, right wing, none of that made any difference to him. He was very cunning; the police, as much as they tried, couldn't find him doing anything blatantly illegal. He always managed to hide behind his employees.

"He had only one weakness. He loved very young blond girls. I was still only a teenager and I looked even younger than I was. I was made for the assignment. I took it. On his pillow, late in the evening after he'd taught me the most horrible things about sex I would ever know, he would tell me his secrets—all

117

of them. I was nothing to him, a mindless little girl with yellow hair. That was all. He had no fear of me.

"He should have. We executed him before I turned sixteen. That was to be the end of it. But it doesn't work that way always. The man had let it be known that I was his. We had been seen often in public in the places where rich men took their paid females. There were many men from those places— and some women—who were very anxious to make sure that a little morsel like myself didn't go unwanted.

"The offers were so amazing and came from such important people that my superiors insisted I take them up. I did. I was passed from one to another person. It's been ten years now. It was easy getting the colonel. I should have a reputation for bringing bad luck to my keepers, but it is a war, and their deaths aren't noteworthy.

"All through it I've had a second life. I would take vacations, people would think I was shopping in Paris, Miami, New York, but I was in training. I insisted on that. I wanted a career. I didn't want to be just another whore for the republic."

"Why are you telling me all this?" Harry was in pain—actual, physical pain. He couldn't get out of his mind the image of a little girl watching her father murdered and her mother raped.

"Because"—she put a hand on his waist in the back, and let it fall down beneath the belt—"I was watching you. You know things. I'm sure of it. You've been through these things. You understand."

There were so many reasons that people have sex. Harry was thinking about them all as he pulled off his clothes. Marty did it to try and prove that he was a man and not a wimp. Cowboy did it for pure hedonism. Beeker did it . . . Harry wasn't sure why the Black Berets leader did it with Delilah, but there was a reason.

And Harry himself? Harry did it to get close to someone. It was the best way he had. He did it to feel, to make someone else feel.

118

All of Angela's story went through his mind as he piled his stuff neatly on the ground. The helicopter had been camouflaged underneath a canopy of cut bush. It was the best—the only—place with any real privacy in the camp. He'd brought Angela here when it was obvious that they were going to do it.

When he'd gotten down to his briefs he stood and watched her. Her back was turned to him as she undid the snaps to her bra. It was a touching act, a final and subtle claim to some kind of innocence that neither of them was sure she deserved. But Harry wasn't going to take it away from her. No way.

Then she bent over to pull off her panties, surprisingly lacy things underneath the masculine military attire she'd worn up to the camp. He almost wished that she'd leave them on. But he wasn't about to ask her to. After the stories, he knew the woman didn't want to be wanted for anything but herself. She didn't want any coy dirty talk about how good she looked in frilly underwear. She wanted to be told that whatever it was that was *her* was something that an honest man would still want.

When she was naked, she finally turned to face him. Her breasts were perfect. They were pale ovals in the moonlight, their whiteness broken only by the wide circles of her nipples. He moved closer, but did it carefully. His chest brushed against hers, delicately.

She put her hand inside his shorts. It wasn't a lewd touch. It was firm, but also strangely appreciative. She wasn't frightened of him.

She lifted her head up to kiss him. As he always did, he felt awkward in this part of the scene. He was always aware of how much bigger he was than the woman. He was aware that he had no protection, no way to hide his arousal, especially not when she was holding him as she was.

She must have sensed his hesitancy. She wanted to be made love to, but she didn't want it to be passionless. She had seen what a big man he was, she had wanted that. She proved it by

119

rolling his heavy muscular body over on top of hers, spreading her legs to let his thick thighs slip in between her own.

Harry started to caress her. There was an immediate moan to let him know she was more than just physically ready for him.

But the stories reverberated in his mind. The tales of the family that had been ruined by the war, the career dictated by the filth of the enemy. He knew what she'd been through; she was right, he knew all about it. Just as much as he wanted to be rid of it in himself, he wanted to rid it in her.

So he made believe he loved her. He made believe that she was the most delicate and most beautiful woman in the world. He lifted up and carefully aimed himself into her belly.

He made it last. He knew he should do that. He held on for as long as he could. She needed a man to give her her own pleasure for once, let her feel the ecstasy of pleasure for herself. He made that all happen and he felt her arms grip the back of his neck, then move up and down his shoulder blades. Only when he was sure she was satiated did he start to move at a speed that was his own.

He was close, he could feel that he was close and that he was going to go over a brink of some kind. She sensed it, too, gripping him harder, her nails scratching, her teeth nibbling at his lips. Then every single part of his body tensed, sending out every part of himself that he could to the woman.

Later she got dressed. He only watched, still sprawled naked on the jungle floor. Was it any good? Had he given her anything?

He didn't know. He just knew he felt something that was better than what he'd been feeling earlier. He could only hope. He could only hope and he could only wonder what was going through her mind.

When she was finished and ready to go—anxious to be back in Cadozza's house in case he went looking for her at dawn—she turned and leaned over to kiss him one more time.

"Thank you" was all she said.

13

This was always Marty's most precious moment.

Until bombs were involved he was just another member of the team. He was the smallest, the least stable, the least attractive, the least everything.

But the minute there were bombs, then Marty became the leader. Marty didn't simply know how to use explosives, Marty *was* explosives. There was no doubt about it in anyone's mind. They always respected his judgment and they always put up with the disgusting way he carried on when he got started.

They were lined up in a clearing in the jungle about 750 yards from the one road that wove through the mountains between Cadozza's camp and the coastal cities. They had used machetes to make the clearing, careful to leave it as shallow as possible. They didn't want it to be obvious to anyone who was traveling on the highway. At this distance it merged into the rest of the greenery if you looked at it.

They had followed Marty's orders exactly and had lined up the five mortars that they'd stolen from their original attackers days ago. There had been ammunition for them, and now they were all set for the next action of the Chequipac Liberation Front.

Marty was being a total jerk about everything. That was no surprise, he always was once you gave him command. But when you're dealing with Leonardo da Vinci, you don't complain about his bad breath or talk about his personality defects, you just mix his paints and you do it exactly the way he tells you to. That's the way the rest of the Black Berets figured it went once they let Marty start to do his stuff.

Marty was acting like a pint-sized white hunter, walking up and down the row of metal tubes that were devastatingly capable of bringing complete death. They looked so innocent, just simple metal pieces of pipe, if you didn't know that there were firing pins at the bottom of the tubes that made a big difference in how the funny-looking rockets acted.

Marty picked up one of the shells now, handling it lovingly. It was the same way a sane man might treat a kitten. He stroked it, cooing to it quietly, speaking to it about the fun times it was going to have.

The shells looked like the plastic rockets he used to buy as a kid. You could fill them up with water and then pump up the pressure until you chose to release them. Then they'd fly like hell into the sky and land hundreds of yards away.

These did the same thing, but they didn't simply end their flight, they had nice charges on them, loads of explosives that would make sure that whoever or whatever was on the other end of the range got a nice long rest from the life he was leading.

"Is he loco?" Amato asked Beeker as they all stood at their assigned places.

Beak grunted. "Just a little bit more than the rest of us."

Amato continued to watch the little man as he put the shell he'd been holding back on top of the carefully constructed pyramid of ammunition he'd constructed. There were four other men: Amato, himself, Beeker, Cowboy, and Harry. As Marty

122

had ordered, each one stood by one of the pyramids. The fifth, they'd all been told, was reserve. On the off chance that one of the mortars wouldn't work, the man with the defective machine was to move over to the standby.

"Now, have you all remembered your lessons?"

Each and every one of them gritted his teeth as he submitted to the little man's schoolmarm tone.

"We're ready, Appelbaum," Beeker said.

"Good." Marty turned his back on them and scanned the part of the highway that was visible. He had his hands clasped behind his back.

"He looks like a washed-out Hitler," Amato whispered to Beeker.

"Jesus! Don't say *that,*" Beeker demanded through his clenched teeth. "He's Jewish. If you talk to him about Hitler, he gets even crazier."

Amato had no intention of bringing up any subject that would make this strange American act any more strangely. He just shook his head and waited with the rest of them.

There was a regular convoy of army vehicles that came up this road at noon every day. Amato had known about it. It was going to be the perfect target. The convoy was run by Cadozza's men. It was an "official" operation, not clandestine in the usual sense, since it was supposedly run by the government's army. But Amato knew that the whole thing was a sham.

The convoy, in fact, was Cadozza's most obvious mechanism for stealing from the government. Those uncontrolled things that could be gotten out of U.S.-supplied warehouses were brought here. There weren't any items of great importance, no sophisticated weapons or parts, but Cadozza made all of his money go farther by using the government's store for the every-day items rather than buying them on the open market.

Instead of using his precious money to purchase canned foods, paper supplies, reading materials, and the like, he just leeched them from the government. With all of the huge problems in El Salvador, Cadozza's petty raids on the warehouses weren't worth anybody's notice.

The sound of the trucks came before any sight of them. They were highballing down the road as hard as they could. The rutted passage kept their speed down to about thirty-five. That was fine by Marty. He'd planned on just that.

He gave a sign and the four men behind him all got in position. He went to the far end of the line where Harry stood and waited with his Greek pal. He thought of this as a moment of glory that he was glad to give his friend. Harry thought it was a pain in the ass to have to be so close to Marty when he was pulling this act of his. But of course, Harry never said that to anyone, certainly not to Marty.

The mortars had been set up and their range calculated as only the wimp could do it. He even had managed to discover a swagger stick some place, a silly-looking piece of braided leather that he was now slapping softly against his skinny thigh.

"Prepare to launch." Marty said it as though he were in charge of mission command at Cape Canaveral rather than standing in a jungle with a small group of men who were about to use some of the least advanced artillery in the modern arsenal. But if Marty was in command of it, they all realized it might as well be a NASA missile. It would be handled just as perfectly.

The trucks were coming closer. The jungle ground was too damp for any dust to mark the convoy's position. Marty didn't need it. He lifted his swagger stick and held in perpendicular to his tiny torso.

Harry swore; he knew how this was going to go. He hated this part of the act as well. But he leaned over and took one of the rockets and held it in his hands. It was nearly two feet long. Harry didn't recognize the type of mortar they were using, he figured it was about 85 millimeter. That would be more than adequate at this range, especially since Marty had set up the damn things. If Marty said they were pointed at the road, they were damn well pointed at the road.

The first vehicle came into view. Marty stared at it through his thick glasses. His mind had ceased to be human. It was computing velocity, angle, distance, firing time . . . he slapped Harry's ass with the stick hard and quick.

Harry dropped his missile into the tube and stood back with his fingers in his ears. It wasn't a question of noise, really. When the shell hit the firing pin at the bottom of the tube, it produced an immediate explosion whose force created an immense surge of pressure all around the tube. Harry wasn't worried about a little loud noise, he was worried about a wave of pressure that could play catastrophic games with his eardrums.

BAM!

The sound of the missile being sent toward its target was loud and quick. No matter how well prepared they were for it, all of them had to jump at the reality when it happened.

The men at the receiving end didn't have the luxury of jumping.

The mortar round hit the front end of the first truck on target. The red-and-orange sight of it got to the Black Berets before the sound; that took a split second longer.

BOOOMMMMM . . .

Marty wasn't waiting to enjoy the spectacle, as much as he would have liked to. He moved to the next man, Cowboy. He had estimated the space between the first vehicle and the second in his earlier calculations. He saw that he was perfectly on target. He slapped the flier's rear with his swagger stick.

Another BAM! sounded as a second missile was sent on its way. This time the explosion was much more delightful. In the short time it had taken to get off the second shell, the fire caused by the first had heated up just enough to ignite the fuel tank of its target. Not only was there the beautiful sound of the rocket—

BOOOOMMMMM . . .

—but there was a synchronized WHOOSH . . . of gasoline as well.

Marty smiled to himself and congratulated nature on improving on his plan. He ignored the activities that were taking place on the road except to note that the third truck was really messing him up. It had stopped too far back. His mortar wasn't aimed correctly.

Going back into his calculating mode Marty saw the correction he had to make and altered the pitch of the third mortar. He stepped back and was about to slap another man with his swagger stick. A harsh reality entered his life.

The next man was Beeker.

Beeker would not like to have his butt prodded to get off a round. Besides, Marty decided with a little frown, Beeker was also a leader of a sort, and deserved some recognition. So Marty just jerked his head once to indicate that all was ready.

The big half-breed snorted and dropped his own rocket into the metal tube. There was the same explosion, followed by another larger one over on the road.

Marty continued up and down the line, getting off four rounds from each of the machines—slapping Harry, Cowboy, and Amato and only shaking his head at Beeker, but making sure that no one forgot that he was in charge so long as the game was artillery.

Ah, and he did it so well. He knew it. He slowed down a little after a while and took it all in. Not one of his rockets had missed. Each one had landed squarely on its target. The first round took out each of the five engines involved—there were four trucks and one automobile in the convoy. The second struck the cargo space; the third was a nice touch, a probably unnecessary cleanup. The fourth was just icing on the cake. Marty believed devoutly in excess.

Perfect. He knew it was perfect. He looked around at the rest of them when he was done and waited for their approval, their admission that he had pulled it off once more.

The bastards weren't looking, though! He started to get really pissed off. They never wanted to give him the recognition he deserved and it made him—

"Get down, you retard, take cover!" It was Harry's voice. What was the problem?

Marty looked back to the scene of his victory and saw that while he might have gotten rid of the convoy, there were some Salvadoran soldiers who were not being so cooperative.

The vista he had seen as only the massive destruction of metal had become alive with death and dying, and also with deadly evidence of the persistence of revengeful men.

All of the truck beds had been covered. It was obvious now that one of them had contained a live cargo of soldiers. Most had to have died in the attack. But some had escaped from the blazing inferno that Marty's perfect aim had caused and were screaming in Spanish for their parents, their loved ones. Some few were calling out a different plea. They wanted a quick visit from the devil to end their agony.

They were the ones who had caught a part of the gasoline tanks on their bodies. There was one who must have been dead. He had to be dead. He was a running, screaming torch, racing through the brush toward them with his entire torso on fire. His arms were upraised, his legs could only be moving through some ghoulish energy that had nothing to do with humanity.

He dropped, finally, only a few yards from the hidden attackers. He never could have seen who had taken his life.

There were others who were less totally enflamed. Their uniforms, their skin, the hair on their bodies, some part of them was being burned off as they desperately tried to save themselves.

They shouldn't even have bothered. Because now Beeker was taking the command. He moved forward, leaving behind the mortar setup, carrying the deadly AK-47 in his hands, ready to do what he knew best. Without hesitation the rest of them followed.

The AK-47's were on automatic. They would be ready. The Black Berets and Amato followed Beeker through the chest-high bush between themselves and the convoy. The Russian weapons had plenty of ammunition, but it was against Beeker's

127

principles to waste it. They held their fire, moving incessantly toward their goal.

As they walked closer, the burning bodies either lost consciousness or else were able to put out their consuming flames. There had only been a very few minutes since the surprise attack had been launched, but these were troops who'd been at war for years. Those who still lived realized that there might be a chance that they could go on living for a while longer if they could get their wits back.

The Berets didn't alter their advance. They were a wave advancing on a beach, impossible to hold back, unthinking in its flow toward the target. Beeker studied the nearly ruined convoy. He was watching for something special. He found it.

There was a leader there. An army in the field never has an ostentatious display of brass and epaulets to show off the rank of its officers. That was for the parade field. In battle, leadership tried to hide itself. Everyone knew that the best way to incapacitate an army was to remove its command. Only a fool would announce the exact location of that brain.

A trained soldier had to find it himself. Beeker had just done that. There was one black-haired man who was shouting orders to the rest. He was good. Beeker would have liked to get a chance to tell him that. He was able to watch the Salvadoran commander ignore the stench of burning human flesh, the destruction of matériel, the panic of his troops. Instead, the guy was barking out the instructions that just might make his group of terrified young soldiers a fighting force again.

Except that Beeker had seen him.

Beeker never would get a chance to sit with the guy and down a few beers. Instead, the half-breed Cherokee stood straight up, taking the chance there was a sharpshooter as good as he was, and let off a short burst of the AK-47 toward the one man who might make things difficult for him.

The bullets cut through the air. They found their target immediately, cutting through his neck, killing him instantly.

As soon as he'd gotten his fire off, Beeker resumed his half crouch in the bush and kept on moving ever closer to the rest of the survivors.

The other men with him had automatically begun to fan out. Beeker was at point, the lead man at the head of an advancing triangle. Marty and Harry were to his left, Amato and Cowboy to his right. He didn't even have to look to know that was true. It was the plan and it was his order. In the field, with men like this, you just take it for granted that they'll do what they'd been told to do.

As they moved, the voices of human beings were more distinct. Someone was sobbing in pain. Beeker knew that sound. It was a terminal pain, the kind that doesn't go away, the kind that you don't wish on anyone, the kind that makes you hope you get to the poor sucker soon enough to put a bullet through his head and end his misery.

Before he could do that, Beeker knew that he and his men had some other business. There was still another man out there who was together enough to be giving orders. The voice was coming from the right. He moved in that direction.

His motion alerted Amato and Cowboy that there was something over there Beeker wanted handled. The three moved closer together and flowed toward Beeker's destination.

There was gunfire to the left. Harry and Marty had made contact and their Russian-made rifles were singing out the praises of some Ukrainian factory worker as they delivered mortal presents to the soldiers of El Salvador.

Beeker let the information enter his head, but he didn't let it distract him. The commanding voice was still talking. He had to eliminate it.

Now they were only a hundred feet from the trucks. The bush was going to end soon. With the evidence of the others' rifle fire to go along with the shock of the mortar attack, the Salvadorans couldn't have doubted the real and continuing danger they were in.

How many were really left? That's what Beeker wanted to know. The more information you had on an enemy, the less dangerous he was. It was the unknown and the unexpected that got fighting men into trouble.

They'd just have to find out the only way they knew how. *Attack*.

Beeker shouted a guttural cry and stood up. He'd gauged the location of that voice and a few others and he let loose with the AK-47 in that direction. Cowboy and Amato were with him, their own rifles carrying just as terrible a tune of destruction.

Beeker never did get to hear the last words that the new commander had spoken, but he could guess what they were. He could sense it, he could feel it. The man had to have been screaming, "Spread out! Spread out!" He had to have because his troops were making the most mortal mistake you can commit on a battlefield. They were letting their fear take over and they were drawing together in a doomed hope that their numbers could mean safety.

The troops clustering together like that only meant one thing: Beeker's job was easier.

His AK-47 was smoking, but he wasn't after all the rest of them, he was after that voice. He let Cowboy and Amato move through the clumped-up young soldiers in the army uniforms as he sought out the one man who was going to be his own special target.

There was no doubt about who it was once Beeker found him. He was a little better protected, a little more calm, a little less flustered, than the rest of them to discover the sudden appearance of this fighting force in front of him.

It didn't do him very much good. When Beeker was finished, he was just as dead as the rest of them.

The stench of death in the tropics isn't any more pleasant just because it's human. Dead meat is dead meat and it spoils quickly in the equatorial sun.

Beeker and the others moved through the ruins of the convoys and gave the last of the men who were breathing the best present they could—the coup de grâce, the bullet that would end the lingering misery of a life after a mortal wound.

When it was finished they realized they had killed twenty-eight men. Already the stench was rising up from the ground. They wanted to leave.

But before they could, Amato had one more job. One final act. He reached into a knapsack he had brought with him and took out a can of white paint and a brush, ridiculous in the context of the devastation that surrounded them.

He used the brush on the still-smoldering hulks of the army trucks. The message was repeated on every one of them, just to make sure no one missed it:

VIVA LA NACIÓN CHEQUIPAC!

14

Rosie thought Cadozza was loosing his cool.

"Who the hell are they!"

Cadozza was storming around the air-conditioned headquarters of his compound. He was in a fury. He was a tall man, six feet, not quite as high up there as Rosie, but no shorty. He was wearing a khaki field uniform; its sharp crease was awfully good proof that he wasn't a man who was going to enjoy a forced march through the jungle terrain that surrounded this compound.

Cadozza's anger was intensified by the very idea that Roosevelt Boone was here to witness the humiliation he had just suffered. This was supposed to have been a pleasant little journey for Rosie and his new friends from El Paso and Ciudad Juárez.

This was like one of those fact-finding things that congressmen were always going on. The kind where they let the fools out of Washington only when everything was just perfect. You don't really show a U.S. congressperson a camp of starving children in Ethiopia, you show him the ones where the kids are actually going to make it.

Kids who were going to make it in Ethiopia were in pretty bad shape, of course, but that was the most that the dummies who ran for office in the U.S. could stand. The ones who had already received their death sentences were too upsetting for men and women used to life on the Georgetown cocktail-party circuit.

Rosie was here in the Cadozza headquarters at the very polite invitation of the commander himself and his ever-friendly partner in capitalism, Uncle Herman Strauss. They'd brought this black drug dealer to El Salvador on a little mission to see just how secure their supplies were.

Rosie knew the gambit: they wanted a big-mouthed nigger to go back to America and talk about the way things were all in control. 'Cept there wasn't much in control in this dump, from what Rosie could see.

"Got you some problems," he remarked casually to the general while he sipped at the tall rum-and-Coke that he'd been served. Rosie had been very careful not to make this sound like an accusation. He simply wanted it to be a comment, an understanding remark from one brother to another.

Cadozza wasn't in the mood for politeness. "There is no problem in this country that I can't handle." The man said it with a viciousness that few would want to argue with.

Rosie studied him some more. Cadozza wasn't bad looking. He had darkly tanned skin, a slim moustache, and his body wasn't totally out of shape, though it showed some wear and tear of the type that was more likely to happen on a nightclub dance floor or a whorehouse than in a war. He was still, somewhere, in there a soldier. He wasn't taking on much of his own product, as there was no sign of the damage that drugs could do to a man.

But the man surely was *agitated*. He was storming around the office with a fury. Rosie waved his now empty glass in the air to signal for a refill. A pretty native woman wearing one of

133

those very full skirts smiled and took the empty container from him. She moved over to the bar that stood at the side of the room and went about the business of making a drink. Cowboy would have liked her a lot, Rosie thought.

Uncle Herman wasn't at all perturbed. He was just furious. He was sitting in a chair near Rosie's with his back at attention so stiff it would have done one of Beeker's jarheads proud on the parade field. He had a fancy cane in between his legs, held in place by both his hands at its top.

Jezebel was the other visitor. She was sitting between her two men, looking worried. Rosie figured she was just concerned because of Uncle Herman's peculiar anger. That must have been something she'd lived with for many years. It must have been frightening for a black girl in America to have been living with —at least near—her German uncle with one of those famous Prussian tempers.

What would chitlins taste like with a side of sauerkraut, Rosie wondered, trying to find a symbolic way to understand the weird schizophrenia that Jezebel must have grown up in.

"It would seem to me," Uncle Herman said through clenched teeth, "that you are the one who should know the answer to your own question. The entire purpose of this exercise was for you to establish a safe location for our operations. This province was supposedly your absolute domain. Now I see that you have no more control over it than you do over anyplace else in your country. What have you been doing? How could you have allowed this stupid little war of yours to interfere!" The cane came down hard on the wooden floor and the sound of its CRACK! made the serving girl jump.

Rosie was pleased, though, that it didn't mean she'd spilled his drink. She now sheepishly carried it across the room and put it in his big black hand.

"Got you some competition?" Rosie asked, trying to make his voice sound helpful.

"No!" Cadozza snapped back. "It's one of those stupid liberation groups that infest El Salvador. They can pop up—"

134

"I really do not care to listen to an explanation about the ludicrous political situation in this country," Herman Strauss announced. "I would much rather listen to you expound on what you expect to do about it."

"How can I fight an enemy that doesn't exist? How can I—"

But Cadozza was interrupted by a new man who entered the office immediately after knocking. He was obviously some sort of trusted aide if he didn't think it was necessary to wait for permission to enter.

"General." The new man saluted his superior.

"This is Major Lucca, one of my staff." Cadozza introduced the officer to everyone at once without bothering to give the major the courtesy of other introductions. The general obviously was anxious to hear whatever it might be that this guy had learned.

The major looked around, anxious about speaking in front of people who were strangers to him. But Cadozza's intent was obvious and so was his anger. This wasn't the moment to give the general a hard time.

"I've spoken to every informant we have. I had our people in the capital go through all the regular army intelligence files. There's no real history of this organization. . . ."

"There must be something," Cadozza insisted.

"There is," the major went on. "The Chequipac are an ancient tribe, long thought to have become extinct with the passing of the Maya. But there was such a tribal group here. Obviously one of the leftist organizations is taking the history of the nation and using it for their own purposes. It could be useful among the truly illiterate ones in the back country."

"Why do you say that?" Cadozza asked.

"The Chequipac were an especially feared tribal group. I spoke to some of the historians and the anthropologists at the university. The legends about them still seem to exist in some of the folklore. In fact, the resilience of the tales about them indicates that some small remnants of the Chequipac may have survived in the high country. There's some indication that

135

might be true. They were vicious warriors. Their religious beliefs were especially terrifying. They had a god who demanded endless human sacrifices and even . . ."

The major stopped and looked at Jezebel. *A gentleman,* thought Rosie, *he doesn't want to upset the lady.*

"Go on! Go on!" Cadozza wasn't being a gentleman and he did not care about a black girl's being upset by disturbing news. *He's really not a nice person,* Rosie said to himself.

"They were cannibals, at least in their rituals. There's some speculation that was the cause of their being wiped out."

"You mean they ate themselves to death?" Rosie laughed out loud.

"Yes, sir," the major actually blushed.

"My, my." Rosie shook his head and his chest heaved with laughter. He wanted to say something to Uncle Herman about the dangers of eating other men, but this just wasn't a laughing group right now, so he skipped it.

"What a ridiculous story," Cadozza said. "There is no such tribe of Indians in our nation. We know all of them."

"But, General, their legend lives on," the major said weakly. "And they may still exist. Many of the isolated areas have ancient tribes that we know little about."

"Your history is too boring for words," Herman Strauss said. "It is not relevant. What is relevant is that someone is interfering with our operations and that the American public, including our customers, believe it's this infernal group whose name I can't even pronounce. Don't you realize that they were on the front page of *USA Today?* That they were reported on the national network newscasts in the United States? They do exist. They must be eliminated."

Rosie had a brief moment of respect for Cadozza when he saw the general's disbelief at Strauss's speech. The man had just said that there was no such tribe in his home country and here was this damn Prussian telling him there was because the American media said there was.

"They haven't actually hurt our system yet," the general

136

said, backing away from the argument about the Chequipac. "They're a chimera right now, something that only appears to exist."

"Things that don't exist do not attack armed camps with the most modern Soviet aircraft, nor do they ambush armed convoys that are supposedly under the protection of a central government force that is supposedly winning a civil war with the help of massive American aid." Uncle Herman was getting very hot under the collar.

"Leave the war to me, Strauss," General Cadozza said angrily. "I'm the one who has to deal with El Salvador after the conflict is over. You should be worried about that as well. The communists are being defeated here. The central government is taking control, American aid is flowing, the Cubans and the Russians are more concerned with Nicaragua than El Salvador nowadays.

"When this damn war is finished, then the government, if we leave it alone, will be in a position of power that could destroy us much more effectively than any guerrilla organization. If there is a strong government with an adequate police force using its control of the professional army, then the kind of enclave we have here will be finished.

"The civil war allowed us to create this little piece of property, you know. Without it we only have two choices: we take over the central government itself, or else we move."

"Moving is out of the question."

"You're right." Cadozza smiled. "And that's the reason you're going to help me stage a coup . . . finally. Forget the little insects that are swiping at us now. The original purpose of our collaboration was political, you should try to remember that. We began this as a means for you to have your damned safety and for me to finance the conservative efforts in El Salvador. You like your money. I like my part of it as well, but I also still intend to become the leader of my country. You need me to win that struggle. You need a friendly government in this country—or would you rather find another host in Latin America?"

"There's nowhere else in the Western Hemisphere where we'll be in such a position as this," Strauss admitted.

For the first time Cadozza was so aware of Rosie and Jezebel's presence that he stopped his loose talk. "I think we'll have to discuss that all later."

"I don't think you like me anymore." All Rosie needed was to have Jezebel pouting at a moment like this.

"Sweet thing, I came all the way down here with you, didn't I? Huh? How can you say things like that to me?" He did his best to sound hurt and disappointed. He knew damn well it always sounded better to women to have a big man like himself put on this act than any other kind of male. They liked to believe that men like Rosie really were capable of being hurt in some way.

"You just sat there looking at that Indian girl the whole time."

"Her? Jezebel, she was the one making the drinks. I am no fool. Of course I was looking at the bartender, that's the reason I looked at you the first time. You were bringing the Scotch, honey."

His honest answer was obviously not the one she had wanted to hear. Rosie could tell immediately that he'd made a drastic error. Her pouting lips protruded even more and she spun around on her heels to face away from him.

They were in the guesthouse of the headquarters. It was a nice little bungalow, but it was too small for the three of them, really. Rosie had no choice. Uncle Herman was staying here with them. Jezebel had made it obvious that the Kraut had a special hold over her sense of morality.

There'd be no chance to make everything all okay later on tonight while he was in the cottage with them. He sighed and began to unbutton his shirt. He had enough experience with Jezebel to realize there was only one way to make her see sense.

She must have understood the sound of the cloth moving around, because she turned just in time to see Rosie finish with

138

the buttons. She smiled a little now. It turned into a full-fledged grin when she saw his hand move down to his zipper.

"You do like me," she said.

Uncle Herman was much calmer when he came and fetched Rosie a couple hours later. Whatever he and Cadozza had cooked up, it made the German more secure about the operations that they were carrying on together.

"Now, after all this unpleasantness, you must come and see the way we do business here in our little compound," Strauss said with his perfect German teeth flashing white through his pale pink lips.

"Delighted," Rosie responded. He'd showered and dressed in fresh clothes after his afternoon romp with Jezebel. The girl was *tiring*. There was no other way to put it. No wonder she'd never gotten herself a regular man in El Paso. She'd have most of the poor devils flat out by the time he found a way to escape from her bedroom. Rosie, needless to say, was up to the challenge, but even he was aware of a little discomfort captured in his jockey shorts. He'd planked the woman three times last night, after they'd arrived, and now he'd had to go twice more in the daytime. What would she demand from him tonight?

These were important considerations. Rosie wasn't at all upset, nor did he think that Jezebel was doing him any harm by making him think about her sexual needs rather than the work in the field. She was work in the field, he reminded himself with a smile. He was just doing all this undercover, and under the covers was as good a way to make his act work as any other.

The two men walked out of the guesthouse and into the blistering hot sun. The compound looked like a movie version of a frontier town; all the structures were built around an empty courtyard. Men and a few women milled about, going about the day-to-day work of any military base, passing time if they weren't on guard duty. There was no sense of urgency here. Rosie assumed that the population had decided that the airborne attack was an aberration.

Too bad, he thought. If Cowboy could do all the damage he was supposed to have accomplished with a single pass of that funny Russkie copter, then it would be great fun to see what he could do if he really tried.

Strauss led the way toward one of the larger buildings. It had once been a church, Rosie knew at once. It had a high steeple and was constructed of the same adobe material that Spanish colonial structures always seemed to be made of.

They walked through the portal and into the building. Inside was a whole lot of stuff that had little to do with religious belief, but Rosie definitely thought it would have a lot to do with penitence when the rest of the team got here.

The church was a veritable warehouse of drugs. He could tell from the acrid smell of cocaine that permeated the air. There was something sweet as well, heroin.

"This is where the supplies are storehoused," Strauss explained as matter of factly as if he were talking about a collection point for the Salvation Army.

"The situation in El Salvador has produced the most beneficial possible climate for us. Cadozza swears that he will take care of the recent annoyances. There have been remarkably few in the years since we began.

"The war here left this part of the country in his powerful and unilateral control. The landing strip is large enough for most private planes and some of the smaller commercial craft as well. With Honduras on full military alert in one direction, Nicaragua in revolt in another, with Guatemala always on the verge of its own communist takeover, the anti-Soviet forces have long been working together to help one another. They have a desirable tendency not to investigate all of their allies' operations too closely.

"They all need money and all of them are involved in some sort of industry that wouldn't make the U.S. Congress very happy."

Rosie looked around at the scene in front of him and realized that there was nothing about it that would make you think that this couldn't be a simple sugar factory. There were big piles of dried marijuana leaves expertly bound together over on one side of the warehouse. There were smaller plastic-wrapped collections of powders that he knew would be the harder drugs. As they talked, there were workers mixing, repacking, and resorting the white dust.

"The United States government has become more difficult about importation of our goods. That has only increased the pressure of demand from the marketplace, as you, a major retailer, know perfectly well.

"But Cadozza's situation has made things incredibly easy for us. First, he is considered a hero by many conservatives in the States. They would do almost anything to keep him in business. Many of them are in high places now. They have proven . . . highly cooperative. If one knows just who will be in charge of a certain customs post at a certain time, then some shipments from friendly countries are allowed to go through the importation procedure very quickly and efficiently.

"For the transport of some of the most expensive of our wares, there is always the opportunity to use a diplomatic pouch, especially if it belongs to a representative of a friendly power. Cadozza has been a necessity for the central government. He has had the ability to fend off the communist guerrillas when others couldn't. His own military force has been highly efficient when the government's was riddled with corruption. In return for his help they've been willing to let his men into places of high power."

Strauss indicated to Rosie that they should leave now. As they walked out of the high door to the church, Rosie couldn't help but be amazed at the vocabulary that Strauss was using.

The old images of dying young people in the black ghetto came back to him. They would be dying because of the poison that had so coolly been described as "goods" by this German. Rosie felt his blood pressure rising. It wasn't a good sign. Rosie knew he was supposed to hold his cool for a lot longer. But he'd get this asshole, he would really get him.

"The raw materials are gathered in other parts of the hemisphere," Strauss continued. "They are manufactured into more easily transported goods, and then they are brought here. That is easy enough. Cadozza has the means to assure the safety of any air or sea traffic entering El Salvador. From here he uses his network of right-wing contacts in other Central American countries and his men in the diplomatic corps.

"Our supplies are assured."

"These redskins that aren't supposed to exist don't make me feel very confident about that," Rosie said, fishing for a reply that would tell him Cadozza's next plan.

"Bah, the savages! The only way for a nation of illiterates like this to be ruled is with a firm hand, one that doesn't shrink from the necessities of discipline and order. The anarchy that democracy allows in these backward places is a disgrace to civilization." Strauss was getting beet red now, and it had nothing to do with the high temperatures.

"So you think your man's going to make it through the night and make sure that I can get some nose candy and some sugar stuff up to the folks in Buffalo?" Rosie asked.

"Oh, yes." Strauss smiled. "He at least understands one important rule of leadership. One doesn't sit around and allow a nuisance to deflect a true leader from his purpose. We'll overlook the annoyance of these small people for now."

They were headed back to Cadozza's headquarters. The guards saluted Strauss; from the way they reacted, they had obviously seen him more than once. He was a regular, all right, there was no doubt in Rosie's mind.

"Ah, my dear, what a pleasure," Strauss exclaimed. Rosie followed his gaze toward the startlingly beautiful woman who was seated on one of the comfortable stuffed chairs in Cadozza's office.

Rosie couldn't keep his lips from pressing together in a silent whistle of appreciation. This was a fine-looking white chick if he ever saw one. And he realized she wasn't just *sitting* on the

142

chair—she was draped over it as beautifully placed as a manne-
quin in a department-store window.

"Mr. Boone, may I present Señorita Angela de la Croix?"
Strauss made the introduction as formally as possible.

"Mr. Strauss, you could introduce your momma if she looks
as good as this," Rosie answered. "How ya doin'?" he asked the
blond woman.

Her tits alone would get her a place in the *Guinness Book of
World Records* so far as Rosie was concerned. They seemed all
the bigger since her body swerved inward after them to a slim
and easily handled waistline. Her short and tight skirt left her
legs visible for his appreciation.

My, my, he thought, *this could be very interesting.*

"Herr Strauss, Mr. Boone, how do you do."

She stood up, and there was nothing Rosie could see in the
full-length version that made him want to change his opinion of
this woman. She was as top of the line as they came and he was
very, very sorry that he had to keep up the game of being
Jezebel's stud. He wouldn't mind giving some service to this
dame any day of the week.

"I understand we have reason to celebrate," Angela said.

"Yes, indeed, I was just about to explain that to Mr. Boone."

"Well, let's do it over champagne, shall we?"

A snap of the fingers brought some native women scurrying
to her. Then there was a barrage of Spanish that Rosie couldn't
really follow. It wasn't necessary, the purpose behind it all became clear soon enough.

They were all sitting while Angela worked the metal restraints on a bottle of vintage bubbly. The cork was pried loose
with a *pop* and the woman proceeded to pour with a sure hand
that made it obvious she was used to this and the other finer
things in life.

When they were all served, she lifted her glass and toasted,
"To the preservation of the republic."

Strauss enthusiastically joined her and Rosie followed course.
He sipped the wine while studying the woman. He was shocked

143

to see her looking right back at him. For a minute he let his sexual fantasies run away with themselves. But, no, he realized. She was looking for something else in him and she had found it.

"I never ask too many questions when someone else is buying the liquor," Rosie said. "But I would like to know what we are doing here."

"It appears that the general and his . . . friends have decided that the moment for their place in history has come."

"Yes, indeed." Strauss was clearly very pleased with a recent turn of affairs. "Our concerns about the supply of your goods to Buffalo are very minor ones now, Mr. Boone. The general has agreed that this is the moment for him to reestablish control of the government of El Salvador."

"The whole shooting match?" This was getting Rosie very interested.

" 'The whole shooting match,' as you so quaintly put it. The concept of a true democracy is something that the American government foolishly thinks can be transported to any other country in the world. It's had its chance here in El Salvador, but the persistence of this minor native group has proven that the central government lacks the ability to control any part of the country.

"There is only one recourse in a situation such as this. There must be a strong man willing to come forward and to take charge of the destiny of his nation. General Cadozza has reluctantly agreed to pick up the torch of civilization."

At that moment the general walked in and saw the trio sipping on the celebratory champagne. He had no doubt what the occasion was and smiled a dictator's smile. El Salvador would be his.

He went over and kissed Angela on the cheek. Strauss obviously enjoyed the scenario and was bursting with his own delight. He was envisioning the future when his goods would be transshipped at the capital's international airport, not from some jungle landing strip.

Cadozza's chest actually seemed to have gotten larger, more inflated with his self-worth. He was going to be the dictator.

Rosie wondered for one moment where Strauss really got his politics. Just what was behind this man's drive? There was something more than money involved here. But then Rosie caught Angela's eye. There was a certain sparkle there that told him the one thing he had already guessed:

Cadozza and Strauss weren't going to make it to the capital. They'd be lucky if they made it to next week.

15

Amato had asked Beeker to come here with him.

The Black Berets leader had agreed without hesitation. The Salvadoran soldier had something he wanted to show the half-breed Cherokee and somehow it would be better if the two of them did it alone.

This was the purpose. It was a small but clear pool of water, remarkably cool for this part of the country. Beeker could see that there was a stream running off from here that explained the perfection of the water.

The two men stood and gazed at the pond and what lay beyond it. "Is that really Chequipac?" Beeker asked.

Amato smiled and shrugged. "It is supposed to be, if you want to believe my grandfather."

Beeker saw no reason to argue. The ruins rose up over the water. They weren't the astonishing things that Beeker knew existed in other parts of the country. They rose to a height that wouldn't be more than two stories on one of today's buildings. But there was a certain grace to their stone construction. It wouldn't have impressed many other people, but Amato was looking at it with an expression of reverence.

Beeker understood that. Whenever he took his son, Tsali, to one of the old Cherokee areas, the two of them had the same reaction. Another man might only see some rough reproductions of transportable hunting lodges or else a strangely unexciting landmark of a place where the Cherokee nation had hidden for decades from the intruding Europeans, but it had been their heritage, the history of a people that others had tried to eliminate but couldn't. The very fact that Tsali and Billy Leaps would be standing there was witness to the perseverance of the Cherokee nation.

So, too, was Amato standing in front of the tribunals of history and telling them to go to hell. All the white man's diseases and all his wars, his corruption, and his ideologies, none of them had been able to erase the existence of a people who lived here first.

The two men didn't speak about such obvious things. They had talked earlier about the lines that made their backgrounds similar. In a previous millennium they might have been enemies, or traders with one another's tribe. But the time when there could be distinctions between the peoples who had the best claim to the Western Hemisphere had ended.

Now, those who had survived had to cleave together. There was no choice. They were the ones who had to retain the history that remained and see that the rituals were not forgotten.

"It's supposed to be a holy place," Amato said, suddenly and strangely shy. "This is supposed to be where the men who would be warriors came to clean themselves before a battle."

That explained the trip, and it also told Beeker why it was just the two of them. They were the Indians. They were the ones who might understand this importance. He stood still for one moment, silently repeating an ancient Cherokee prayer that the men used before they went to meet their foes. With his own ancestors having gotten their due, Beeker began to strip. He'd give Amato's their due as well.

When the two men were naked, Amato walked into the water, chanting in a language that reminded Beeker of some of the tongues he'd heard in Asia. He couldn't understand the words and didn't ask their actual meaning. Their intent was obvious.

He walked into the cool water after Amato. It sent some shivers up his skin as he went in to thigh depth.

When they were up to their waists, Amato stopped. He lifted up his arms and threw his head back, the surge of his language increased, the pace of the words and the loudness of his cries went out over the jungle with enough impact to send the multicolored birds screeching for refuge.

Then Amato suddenly dived in. Beeker followed. They swam across the still pool till they struck the rock of the ruins. Then they walked up out of the water. Silently they marched up the rough steps to the apex of the timeless structure. Amato sang out more of the hymns of his almost forgotten people. Beeker was beside him, hoping his parade-rest stance was a sufficiently reverent proof of his respect.

Then Amato stopped. The two of them stood naked on the temple structure and were quiet. "Thank you," the Salvadoran finally said.

"For giving me the honor of being able to worship with your ancestors?" Beeker scoffed. "I'm the one who should be thanking you."

They walked back down to the bottom of the steps. Beeker wouldn't have minded entering the pool again and feeling once more the sensual relaxation the swim had given him. But Amato carefully walked around its edge. When they were pulling their clothes back on, he explained:

"The warrior can enter the holy water only when he is about to go to battle. Once he has consecrated himself to the gods, he cannot enter it again until he's proven himself on the field of valor. The waters of this temple are over the place where the great warriors of the Chequipac are buried. It would be a horrible desecration if any but a tried and proven man were to enter them."

Beeker nodded. Someday, he thought, Tsali would have to come here and swim. Then he realized that he hoped that he and Amato would be around to do the honors themselves.

16

"Darling, what does your Uncle Herman get out of all this?" Rosie and Jezebel were naked in bed, as usual. He thought he'd asked a fairly straightforward question, but he couldn't help notice the way her body stiffened. Uncle Herman had a grip on her and he just wasn't sure what the story was here.

"Money." It was a simple answer, but Rosie didn't believe it. Just the curt way she spoke proved to him that there was something more.

"After a certain point a man doesn't need more money. Some guys are strange that way, like they want to be King Midas and collect all their gold—"

"Uncle Herman does like gold," Jezebel broke in. "He and my daddy learned they couldn't trust all the paper stuff in the war in Europe. They came out of that with nothing but my momma's marriage license to save themselves. They vowed they'd never be in that place again."

"Yeah, I can get that," Rosie said. "But what does your uncle

150

want more for? He doesn't have any kids, and it sure looks like he's never going to."

"Don't talk about that!" Jezebel sat up quickly. "You just forget my Uncle Herman."

"I can hardly be expected to forget about a man who I'm supposed to be giving a couple million dollars' worth of business to. I'm not a fool, woman. I just was asking what makes the man tick."

"Things you wouldn't know about. Things you should just leave alone. Uncle Herman's an honest businessman and he'll keep his promises to you. Wasn't he willing to bring you down here to see the operation yourself? That should be proof enough for you that Uncle Herman is a fine German, a fine—"

Rosie surrendered. "Okay, okay. I don't know why a brown baby like you is so happy to have a Kraut uncle, but if you are, you are."

He stood up and began to pull on some clothes. "Gonna take a walk," he said.

"Now you're mad at me." She began to pout once more.

"No, no. Leave it alone, woman. I just want to take a walk. This little siesta was a fine idea, but it's over now. I want to catch some fresh air, see what's going on."

"I'm going to stay here," she responded. "I'm still tired."

"You have a right to that," Rosie muttered.

"What did you say?"

He leaned over and kissed her forehead. "I just said you should have yourself a fine little nap, sweet thing. You just rest your pretty body and get it ready for some more good times tonight."

Rosie strode through the plaza of the compound. Once this was a little farming village, a marketplace for the surrounding peasants to come and do their trading. But there was nothing left of what was once called Domingo.

The church was a chemical factory. The governor's palace was a military headquarters. The few women were in uniform or else they were camp followers, the omnipresent whores who kept up any army's morale.

No one found Rosie's presence that interesting. Maybe they were used to having Americans like him around. There certainly could have been others who were dressed like him, with gold chains over exposed chests, tight pants with Italian zippered boots and metallic sunglasses. Here, in the middle of a military zone, no one was even paying any attention to his shaved head.

He moved over to the scene of the most activity in the area. "What's happening, man?" Rosie smiled at one of the men who were working hard at setting up a clearing.

Luckily, he happened on one of the Salvadorans who understood English, not that rare a commodity down here after waves of American advisors, mercs, and media people, let alone the hundreds of tourists who'd been coming here for years before that.

"Setting up the place for General Cadozza's little present."

"Oh?" Rosie couldn't figure out the joke.

"We're going to get a new defense system. Those damned communists won't be able to get through this with their Russian helicopters by the time we're finished."

"That's great, that's just great." Rosie laughed. He didn't want to ruin the man's day by letting him know that any anti-aircraft defense was going to be useless against a man like Cowboy, even if it did get installed in time to give the flier some problems.

Rosie walked on, moving toward the governor's palace, wondering if he might get a chance to talk to Cadozza for a bit alone. Who knew what the asshole might spill if he was talking to a man he thought was just another black gangster from some unknown city in the far north?

But as Rosie came closer he could see the blond woman. She was dressed in an outfit that was so stylish it clashed with the surroundings. Her skirt was slit in an oriental fashion that left the tops of her thighs exposed—and very nicely, too, Rosie thought. Her blouse was a pale peach color, just perfect for her slightly tanned skin. You could barely see where the fabric ended and the flesh began—not a bad image, since it implied a nudity that Rosie wouldn't mind getting a chance to judge for himself.

But the lady was already engaged. She was talking quickly to a man in military dress, and the way she was speaking to him with her hands and constant sweeps of the area to see who might be overlooking their rendezvous certainly didn't seem to have much to do with Cadozza's bedroom. That was the only thing that Rosie had thought the lady had to do in the outfit. At least so far as anyone was supposed to really know about.

He had his doubts, though. The expressions they had exchanged the other night had been loaded with meaning. Rosie had left the rest of the group before they could get straight on what kinds of codes and passwords they'd use on this campaign, other than the really obvious ones, those that they'd use with one another in the strictest confidence. Rosie didn't expect this lady to have one of them to use, but maybe she could show her hand in another way.

The soldier was walking away swiftly by the time Rosie came up to Angela. She saw the black American approach and smiled. "A warm day," she said when he was within hearing.

"That it is," he agreed. Rosie made no attempt to hide his very impressed reaction to a close-up look at Angela. There was no bra underneath the peach blouse, and that meant he could see quite a bit.

"We have friends in common, Mr. Boone. I don't think they really expected you to be in quite this place."

"Oh?"

"Yes." She looked at him intently. But Rosie wasn't going to bite with only that kind of come-on. She could sense it. She seemed to do some quick thinking, all the while scanning the area for any eavesdroppers. She smiled quickly; she'd found a way to communicate to him effectively. "Yes, Tsali would be

153

very surprised to know that his friend Rosie was here in Domingo."

Rosie had to hand it to the woman. He was remembering the old stories about the American Indians who were used to pass on information over the radio wires during the Second World War. Try as they could, no matter how good the Germans and the Japanese were at breaking a scientific code, there was no way they could decipher Navajo or Choctaw when it was spoken over the battlefield radios.

Tsali, that was just as good. There was no mistaking that. It wasn't the kind of thing that anyone could have learned easily. The kid was back in Louisiana taking his turn as the guardian of the homestead, the house and farmland that Beeker had long ago decreed could never be left unguarded.

"Yes, well, I suppose then that we do have some awfully good friends in common. I take it your little, uh, chat just now was something to do with them."

She nodded. "The general's not only planning an assault on the coast—you know that, you heard it as well as I did. He's arranged for some of the most sophisticated missiles to be brought here in case the helicopter returns. I've just sent a message that now is the time. You agree?"

"I certainly have no problem with that schedule. I could sure take a rest from little Jezebel."

"What have you discovered about them? Strauss is a regular visitor here. He's more than just another one of Cadozza's drug connections."

"For a while, at least, that's where we're going to have to leave it," Rosie said. He didn't like it, but there wasn't any more to it than that. "We got bigger problems, anyway. You and me are going to be in the middle of a big load of trouble if you've told the boys it's time for them to come visiting. You have any thoughts about where we should be?"

"Oh, yes." She smiled. "I have some very definite ideas about the safest and most important place for the two of us. I've

154

suggested they move tonight, after midnight. We're all having dinner. Perhaps you and I could arrange to meet after that."

"Easy enough. Old Jez doesn't like to do the dirty deed when her uncle's around. They'll be tucked in snug as bugs by that time of night. You and me will have a very easy time getting together. Very easy. You do have some little items that would make it a more interesting event, I hope."

17

They were getting ready.

Angela's information had gotten to them earlier in the day. Now it was night. There wasn't that much of a march to Domingo. They could make it easily and not tire. Other men might, but not them. They were trained for just this kind of thing.

They sat now and did their rituals. Another time, another group, and those rituals might be different. But these were the ones that had meaning for the Black Berets. Too much meaning. They'd gone through them too often.

Cowboy stood and watched Harry and Marty as they prepared. The uniforms had been made by an old Indian woman whom Beeker had found. Their camouflage material would make it easier for them to melt into the night. They had already put on the pants, the shirts, the specially made boots. Now came the painting.

It was awesome. Every time he'd seen it and every time it'd happened to him, Cowboy had felt a chill move up and down his spine just like the one he had now. There was no way around it.

The two men, the big Greek and the little runty blond man, were seated on the ground facing one another. They had their greasepaint out. First, Harry dug his thick fingers into the can and brought out the stuff. It was dark, smeared with waves of different colors. He painted it onto Marty's face, leaving areas only around his eyes, which now appeared to be startlingly pale blue.

Then, Marty took his turn. He spread the paste over Harry. As he did it, the Greek's face seemed to disappear. He just went into the night. It was frightening, that's all, just frightening.

But the worst was when they were finished. Because then they stood up and they walked toward Cowboy with those cans of cammy grease in their paws. It made a man feel like crying, just bawling like a baby. They were ghouls, vampires of the night coming to get him, to turn him into a machine of destruction, something less than human—or was it more than human? Who ever knew?

Whenever this happened, Cowboy had a visceral desire to flee. This wasn't what a nice boy from Oklahoma was supposed to go through. No way. He was supposed to be home and comfortable in his bed, he should be living with his six-pack a night, his woman, his babies. He shouldn't be standing here and passively allowing these creatures to approach, their hands outstretched, ready to turn him into something he wasn't.

But he didn't move.

They came up to him and then they both reached up with their fingers. Men never touched Cowboy this way. Never. Not with this softness, this care and concern. But here were these . . . creatures who were so delicately painting his face, preparing him to join them. He could do nothing but close his eyes and let it happen.

Beeker had seen it dozens of times, maybe hundreds. He still couldn't stop watching it. He wondered if he should explain it to Amato. But, no, of course not. The man was trained by the Marine Corps. He understood. The Salvadoran was standing beside him. Beeker turned, but before he could say anything, Amato had sat down on the ground and beckoned Beeker to join him.

"The jaguar is the only animal in the world that hunts human beings for food. Did you know that?" Amato asked as he dug into his pack. "Others will attack a man if they feel threatened, or if they're starving. But to the jaguar, man is only another competitor, one who must be eliminated.

"The jaguar is the totem of the Chequipac. We become him to secure his skill and also to assure ourselves that we will be as bloodthirsty as he. The weak do not survive in the jungle. The man who would be less strong than the jaguar is doomed.

"We will survive because we will take the spirit of the jaguar into ourselves."

Amato had U.S.-issue cammy grease, just the same as the others', in his hand now. He dug into it and brought out a glob of it on his fingertips. He moved his hand to Beeker's face and rubbed it in careful stripes across Billy Leaps's forehead.

"Forget the modern ways," Amato intoned. "This is the way of our ancestors. I am not putting anything manufactured on you. I am anointing you with the spirit of the jaguar. You are becoming him."

Billy Leaps Beeker believed it. He felt a strong feline inside him. He sensed his eyesight becoming stronger, more focused and piercing in the darkness. He had never considered himself graceful, only capable when it came to moving across a field under enemy fire. But now, he was a cat. A big cat. His muscles flexed with their ability to propel him fluidly in any way he desired. He looked up for some unconscious reason and saw the tall jungle trees. He could climb them without rope. For this one moment he honestly believed that. And he could jump down from their tops without harming himself.

There was no concern if he did find himself damaged. He

158

looked down to Amato and realized his fellow warrior was giving him a gift of extra lives.

He wanted to yowl, to snarl his intentions to his enemy. He wanted to feel his fingernails. Somehow he was sure that they'd become claws.

But Emanuele was waiting. He had finished. It was Beeker's turn. The Black Berets leader picked up the can, which felt suddenly alien to him. But he knew what he had to do with it.

He took the colored grease on his own fingers and transported it to Amato's face. He had always used this ritual of preparing for battle as a serious and solemn occasion. But this time it was even more so. He was giving his friend the extra lives that a warrior would need when he faced a dangerous enemy.

When he was finished, Beeker stared deeply into Amato's eyes. He would never know if it was true, if it was possible, but he swore to himself that they'd changed color and shape. They were cat's eyes now. The Chequipac lived. The Chequipac had committed the rituals of the jaguar. The Chequipac were ready to hunt their enemy, mere mortal men.

They had marched up to the perimeter of the camp. They knew from Cowboy's first attack that their maps of its layout were accurate. They had each memorized the positions of the buildings that had once been the village of Domingo and were now the headquarters for Cadozza's doomed army.

Nothing had allowed Beeker to get back his old self after the rites he had undergone with Amato. He no longer fought it. It felt good. It felt more than good. It was awesome. He was a killer now. Whatever there might have been at one time to make him want to resist the transformation no longer existed within him.

The medicine of the Chequipac had taken. There was a thirst for blood in his system. He spied on the perimeter of the camp. There was a single guard lounging around there.

Usually it would be Harry who would take him out. But

Beeker wanted this one himself. He gave no order to the others, but instead reached inside his belt for the razor-sharp, six-inch-blade, military-issue knife that was one of his favorite weapons.

He moved stealthily on the guard. He was a jaguar. A cat. There was no noise. There was no warning. His mind was altered so completely that he didn't think he attacked the man, but that he *sprang* at him. With one move that he would never have thought to make at another time, Billy Leaps Beeker was airborne. His blade was his paw, its steel was his claws, the guard was his prey.

The knife slashed out and sliced the man's neck, at the point where the jugular lay just beneath the skin. There was no sound because there was no voice box left to function. The cut had been that deep and that penetrating.

Beeker looked at the dead body in front of him and felt nothing. It was the fate of the man who would intrude on his lands.

The others followed. They knew that total silence was necessary for them to succeed, but Harry wanted desperately to say something to Beeker. He had watched the attack on the sentry and he'd never seen anything like it. He had no choice but to thrust Billy Leaps while they were in the middle of an operation, but the leader was attacking strangely.

Now they had to wait. Harry's assignment took him to the far side, away from Beeker. He was nervous about it, but there was no way to alter things now.

Soon, right on schedule, they heard the drone of the Russian helicopter as it approached. Harry forgot about Beak and focused on the pretty tune that Cowboy was playing instead. The rotars of the Hind-D were making a wonderful symphony all their own. At least it was wonderful for the Black Berets. Harry had never been on the receiving end of one of Cowboy's songs, and he didn't ever intend to be.

The arrival of the helicopter was their signal. Delilah's presents included some wonderful toys that they'd never seen before: BG-15 grenade launchers. There were enough for each man to turn his AK-47 into a fine piece of field artillery. Each one of them had one of the eleven-inch accessories to add to his rifle. Each one had a nice set of 40-millimeter grenades to go with the launchers. With a range of at least four hundred yards and an ability to kill anything within a five-meter radius of impact and maim any unfortunate man or animal within up to twenty meters, this was going to be a very unpleasant surprise for the troops who were defending Cadozza's little fiefdom.

The copter moved closer now. They could hear shouts in the compound. The alert was taking place. The targets were better identified this time, but Cowboy couldn't see them as clearly. No problem. Their first round with the BGs wasn't going to be one of the lethal ones. Instead, they all had flares loaded up and ready to lead Cowboy to his deadly destinations.

As soon as the machine was above them, Beeker started the action. As soon as the rest of them saw his flare flying through the air, they let loose with their own. For a full minute the central square of Domingo was lighted as well as Giants Stadium. It was all the time that Cowboy needed.

The Hind-D swooped down and began to send out its fearsome missiles. The church was the main target. They wanted to eliminate any possible source of wealth for any man who was part of this operation. Even a small bag of the refined heroin could have made a survivor a millionaire by the time he got it to a city street—but they knew now he wouldn't.

The missiles found their target, exploding the old Spanish structure to pieces. One after another the Russian rockets made their way through the night sky and found the church.

The fires that resulted were all the flier would need for the rest of his work. They could forget playing with flares. It was time to screw in the fun things.

The BGs had a wicked kick to them. They'd learned that by getting their shoulder muscles sore testing out the Russian weapons. Harry braced himself as he aimed his at the back door to the governor's mansion, the score he'd been especially assigned.

He pulled the trigger and the damn thing bucked back on

him, hurting him a lot but not enough to keep him from getting the next round ready. There wasn't any time for delay and he knew it.

On every side of him there were echoing explosions as the rest of the team got off one after another of the devastating Russian grenades. In the village under the illumination of the burning church the bodies of the Salvadorans were piling up and the screams of dying men were filling the air.

Domingo was a mass of confusion. There were orders being yelled out in Spanish all around. It wouldn't do them any good. The Black Berets had begun to move in on the command post.

The BGs had not only taken care of any man who had come anywhere close to the back door of the governor's mansion, they had utterly destroyed the whole of the building around the doorway. Harry was able to walk straight through it. His AK-47 was on automatic, no longer burdened with the grenade launcher, back to its usual deadly use.

He stepped over the rubble at the door and moved into the first room. There were only corpses to greet him. He wished he had the time to at least roll down the eyelids of the dead men who were staring lifelessly into space, but there wasn't a chance for that kind of touch now.

Especially not now.

Harry stepped to the side, his rifle ready, when there was a sudden burst of automatic fire behind him. As he swiveled to face it, his fingers ready, he caught sight of something in the next chamber. He could only let it register for a moment. It was an armed man and he was racing toward Harry with something ominously metallic in his hands.

There comes a time when every man who fights knows that he's finally taken the long count. Harry had that flash. He was trapped, the doorjamb was too shallow to give him any protection. The most he could do was take as many of the others with him as he could, to leave fewer for the others to have to face.

The AK-47 was ready. He pulled the trigger and held it on automatic. Harry didn't miss often, but there were at least five

162

men who'd made it through to his rear. He was going to have to be superhuman to get them all. When he had, there was no way he would have time to take care of the unknown force on his other flank.

The AK did its work. It sent out a wave of molten lead into the air in a clean line that swept the fivesome as they approached. They just weren't as good as Harry. That was all. They just weren't as fast, as accurate, or as lucky. Because their rounds didn't find their target. Harry's did.

It wasn't his cleanest kill and he knew that at least one of them had only been incapacitated. But it'd have to do. He had to at least try to turn as quickly as possible and take out the ones on the other side.

Harry moved on his heels and the burning-hot barrel of the AK-47 pointed into the farther room. Then he froze. Instead of rifles firing, there was only silence to greet him. That, and the sight of two men who were very dead.

Standing over them, still holding on to the pistol that had cut them down, was Angela. His blond goddess was smiling at him.

Marty had watched as Cowboy went about his beautiful business. He was pissed. Once again Cowboy had the fun stuff, the big bangs. Here he was, the one they all knew perfectly well was the best at the most dangerous and most demanding work with the biggest explosions, and he was reduced to playing around with some little-kid grenades that were launched from a goddamn peashooter. It was a waste of talent. That was the only way to put it. It was a goddamn waste of talent.

Cowboy was purposely going after all the vehicles that were left in the open after he'd taken out the church. That was the plan. The big cannon that were mounted on the Hind-D were perfect for it, capable of destroying any hope the Salvadorans might have that they would be able to ride out of the place.

There was another purpose to it. Cars and trucks that remained all had fuel in them. The tanks provided convenient and disruptive explosions, often destructive enough that they could take out a few men with them when the recurrent *whoosh* let the attackers know that another had been hit.

Marty surveyed the scene and got even madder. He was all prepared to go gung-ho into the middle of everything and show them just what he was made of. He wanted to make a big grandstand play. Run into the middle of the village square and stand there, his rifle blazing, as he took on all comers, proving to everyone that he had the balls to do it. But, *damn,* there went Beeker and Amato doing just that very thing!

Damn! No one ever doubted that Beeker was brave. But here he was, pulling something that he'd tell Marty was only a stunt. The two of them, the two redskinned idiots, were standing with hardly any cover, back to back, their rifles spitting out endless rounds of ammunition at any Salvadoran who was stupid enough to approach.

Damn! They were all taking away his fun.

Someday, all these fools were going to get Rosie killed.

There was no way to get a message to the rest of the Berets to let them know just where he was going to be. He and Angela had figured that the guesthouse wouldn't be one of the targets. He could only hope that the crazy chopper jockey up there in the sky who seemed intent on blowing away half of Central America with his cannons wasn't going to be so enthusiastic as to go after the small structure Rosie was headed for.

Angela wanted to take out Cadozza herself. That was their plan. That meant that Rosie was going to get the pleasure of giving Uncle Herman his own farewell. They were to finish their assignments and then meet back at the general's hiding place. The crooked Salvadoran had been kind enough to keep all of the gold he insisted on being paid with in one single place. They knew there was no way for Cadozza to get it all out of Domingo. But they also realized it was in a location secure enough that once they had taken care of the general and the Kraut it was the best place for them. Besides, there'd be some other hotshots in the outfit who'd know what was going on and

164

might want a chance at the cache themselves. They had to make sure that didn't happen.

Rosie was carrying one of the trusty M16's that Cadozza had been given by the U.S. Rosie was glad to have such a familiar companion on his little journey.

He made his way through the small village. He'd become familiar enough over the past few days so that none of the troops were worried about him. They seemed all to recognize him or to decide that a flashily dressed black man wasn't their problem in the middle of this surprise attack.

Rosie got to the house and didn't bother with the politeness of a knock. Even if he had, the sounds of the battle outdoors were too extraordinary for any fist on wood to be heard.

The black man kicked in the door. He was ready for a confrontation with the Kraut. But there was no German there. Well, there was a half Kraut, Jezebel. Rosie immediately knew he made a mistake when he put down his rifle. He knew it because Jezebel didn't put hers down.

"Woman, why are you pointing that at me? I came here to defend you," Rosie lied. He stared down the sights of the female's own M16.

"Anyone comes in here, I'm supposed to kill him, or keep him captive till Uncle Herman gets away."

Jezebel wasn't going to budge from that stance, Rosie could tell. "Why do you think that your white man uncle is going to be able to get away in this mess?"

"He's gotten away from worse, when he was a little boy he had to get out of worse things than this. I know all the stories, the ones him and my daddy told me about Germany and how they suffered and had to run all the time. But this time Uncle Herman's got the money to make it easy."

"There is not enough money in the world to make this easy, you little fool. There is a *battle* going on outside. There are troops, there are guns, there are no vehicles left."

"Uncle Herman never does go anywhere he can't get out of himself. I told you, he learned his lesson."

165

They weren't going to go anywhere. Rosie understood tha
He also knew what it meant that the fire outside was becoming
more sporadic. One side or the other was winning. He had few
doubts which one that was. He put his rifle down and sat on the
couch.

"Leave that alone, woman. Come over here and sit down.
Tell me some of your stories about Uncle Herman. I'm very
interested."

18

"Now, this is the way a man should live," Rosie said to no one in particular.

They were sitting in lounge chairs that lined the deck near the swimming pool at the most expensive resort hotel in Key West. The sun was hot and the drinks were cold.

"Tequila," Cowboy said softly, "endless amounts of tequila."

"And girls!" Marty would have to bring that up. "There's more skirt here than anyplace else in the world—and they *want* it, you all know they just want it." He grotesquely grabbed hold of his crotch through his swimming suit.

Everyone hoped that he'd shut up if they ignored him long enough. But he had to keep on going. "Don't you guys pull that on me. Just because you got laid all the time down in El Salvador, it doesn't mean that the rest of us can't get it up here in the good old U.S. of A. Hell no, Tsali and I have as much right to a piece of ass as the rest of you, isn't that right, kid?"

Even if the mute Tsali could have responded, it was doubtful he would have. He stayed in his chair, tasting the good lime taste of the authentic Margarita that his friend Cowboy had bought for him, and just smiled at the sun.

"I'm not at all sure it was such a hot thing to have a woman like that Jezebel. *Je-sus,* she did really know how to handle that rifle."

"What was her story, Rosie?" Cowboy lifted up his sunglasses and turned to the huge bulk of his black friend.

"Too strange to tell, son, just too strange. She had her a German daddy. Now, you would certainly think that anyone with a mind would understand that the fact you had a black momma was more important in this world. But ole Jezebel just loved her daddy. I think she loved him too much and in some strange ways. And she loved her uncle.

"Seems the two brothers weren't exactly blameless in the old days. Herman would have been too young to really have understood or have done all that much. I guess he might have been one of those Nazi boy scouts. . . ."

"A Hitler *Jugend?* You mean your black girlfriend was a Nazi?" Marty was getting upset with the subject; they all should have known he would be.

Rosie tried to calm him down. "I have no facts, mind you. I just know that there's lots of suspicions there. Seems that Uncle Herman was the other half of Cadozza's brains. He was smart enough that he kept his own air transportation nearby just in case something happened just like what did happen. Cowboy didn't have lights enough to see the other copter getting away. I think we might just meet up with that asshole again someday. I just got that feeling."

"Hey, and you, Harry? You going to meet up with that blond chick again, or you going to give me a chance to prove my stuff?" Cowboy directed the conversation away from the dangerous implications of discussing Nazism in front of Appelbaum.

"I don't know." That was all Harry ever was going to say about Angela in front of these guys. But inside? Well, maybe there'd be another chance. She was something, he thought.

168

Someone who was able to take care of herself and play all the games, but still had that little flicker of humanity. He only hoped he had one inside him. If it was there, maybe it took a woman like Angela to get it burning brightly.

"God knows, the woman helped with Tsali's education," Cowboy joked. He was the team's accountant, the one who kept tabs on the money. The caper in El Salvador certainly hadn't hurt their finances. There was a delectable pile of gold that was wondrously untaxable as it sat in a few scattered safe deposit boxes around the country, with just a little bit in Switzerland for a rainy day. The thought helped Cowboy forget that he was one of the few who hadn't found a sexual outlet, a fact that hurt all the more since that was Latin country, his home base for love and lust.

They were quiet for only a little while before Marty broke the silence again. "What happened to Beeker that night? Him and Amato just disappeared when it was all finished. They weren't around for the cleanup or anything. Last thing I knew they were in the square playing come-and-get-me suicide games and then . . . poof! Off they went."

"It was just an Indian thing." That was all Harry wanted to say about Billy Leaps Beeker's strange behavior that night.

"Then he must have told you about it, Tsali. Come on, kid, what did your old man say?"

The young Cherokee was still for a moment. Then he began to sign. Marty slapped Cowboy's arm to get his attention. Appelbaum had never learned the hand lingo as well as the pilot had, and Marty wanted a translation.

Cowboy spoke slowly; it was obvious that some words were difficult and that Tsali was spelling them out, knowing that even Cowboy wouldn't have them in his vocabulary.

"They went to wash away the spirit of the jaguar."

"Like I told you," Harry said, "it was an Indian thing. Someone find a waitress. I need another drink."

"Well, I think something strange's going on. Where'd Beeker go?"

"He told you, he went fishing."

"Fishing! If he went fishing, why'd he just take Delilah? Huh? You tell me. Why didn't he take the kid? He always takes the kid fishing when he goes."

"Leave it alone, Marty. The man wanted to go out fishing with his girl. What's the big deal?" Cowboy was trying to deflect still another conversation now.

"He said he went fishing for sharks. Why does he want to fish for sharks in Florida?"

"Just leave it alone, Marty."

"I used to be able to use a boat like yours for fishing, myself. But then came the time when I would have to have one like this follow me. At least one. Then the fun was gone. It's one of the things I miss."

Beeker was surprised that he spoke English so well. Then he remembered that he'd gone to college in the United States, even been scouted by one of the major league baseball teams. It made sense. The half-breed Cherokee sat in the lounge chair that was set up on the deck of the Cuban destroyer somewhere in international waters between Havana and Key West.

The man was also bigger than he'd thought. They sat silently while a uniformed waiter brought them rum and juice drinks. The man toasted Beeker silently. The Black Berets leader returned the gesture.

"They told me that you wouldn't believe anyone else but me. On the one hand, I think that's pigheaded of you. But, then . . . I was flattered. I know about you, Beeker. You have quite a record. It's a strange one, and in some ways terrifying. But always admirable in terms of honesty and raw courage. I salute that in a man. I think I had it once, in the mountains, before all this." He waved his fat cigar at the entourage that surrounded him.

"Yeah, I figured you did have it. That's why I wanted to talk to you, face to face."

"They say you want my pledge that . . . the same thing

170

happened in Colombia. The papers are full of it. Isn't that enough?"

"Headlines mean shit nowadays," Beeker responded. "All I know is a bunch of guys who didn't know anything about world politics had to be taken out of El Salvador because they were stupid enough to think that a man they thought was their leader was clean, honest. He wasn't. But they were the ones who had to pay for it."

"The damage you inflicted on the camp at Domingo was . . . significant," the man agreed, puffing his cigar.

Then he looked out over the calm sea. He put the cigar in his mouth and talked with it clenched between his teeth. "There are peasants in the mountains of Colombia who thought that a certain group of people who had been trained in my country were going to lead them in a glorious revolution.

"Those illiterate peons had proven their valor over and over again. They had gone to war against the capitalists who enslaved them. But"—he shrugged—"their leaders became greedy. They lost sight of their revolutionary goals and instead realized that the cocoa leaves that had been financing their campaigns would also finance their decadence in the capitals of the world.

"The papers are—for this one time—correct." The man threw his cigar overboard, an obvious disgust taking hold of him. "For once, the Colombian government forces were able to infiltrate the rebel stronghold. For once, they had competent generals and sufficient supplies. For once, the Colombian troops didn't steal the drugs that were stockpiled, but burned them.

"The world knows this is true because only the most modern and advanced American airships were used in the attack that made sure that not only were the leaders of the rebel forces dispatched, but so, too, were all possibilities of a force capable of taking advantage of any structure or war matériel that was in place.

"Many, many men were killed in the Colombian government campaign, Beeker. And if you think that those idiots in Bogotá could have pulled that off . . . ." He was getting angry and sensed it. He stopped himself. "There are many martyrs to the revolution in Colombia these days. Innocent dead."

"Thanks." Beeker stood and took Delilah's arm. "That's all I wanted to hear. There are martyrs for El Salvador's democracy too. Good men. I'll remember to pray for them."

"Pray for the governments of Colombia and El Salvador. They'll need your good wishes. Or pray for yourself, Beeker. You'll need prayers if we ever have to meet in battle."

Beeker had stood and had his hand on Delilah's elbow. He was seeing the dictator's megalomania now. He wasn't surprised. He'd expected this. He believed he'd heard the fighting man's word of honor before. He had to hear it. It had become important to him. But this was just the usual political garbage. Beeker wasn't having any of it.

He led Delilah to the gangplank that went to their rented fishing boat. They'd go back to Key West now and he'd take her and Tsali out for a conch dinner. But he couldn't resist one last line: "If we do meet, watch out for the jaguar."

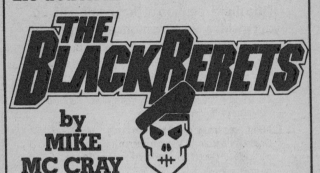